The Library
Union Street
Wells BA5 2PU

C000041085

Stig

Shelve under Grubb.   SOWLS

Please return/renew this item by the last date shown
on this label, or on your self-service receipt.

To renew this item, visit **www.librarieswest.org.uk**,
use the LibrariesWest app, or contact your library.

Your borrower number and PIN are required.

LibrariesWest

1 3 1756729 4

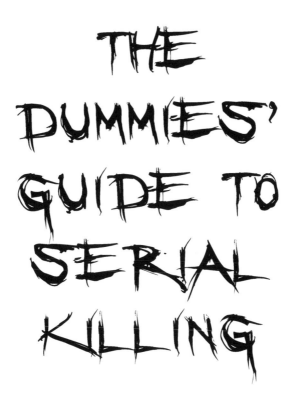

THE DUMMIES' GUIDE TO SERIAL KILLING

And other Fantastic Female Fables

First Published 2018 by Fantastic Books Publishing

Cover design by Gabi

ISBN (eBook): 978-1-912053-86-5
ISBN (paperback): 978-1-912053-87-2

To fantastic women
past, present and future.

Acknowledgements

This collection would not have been possible without the hard work and dedication of the predominantly female Fantastic Books Publishing editorial team who work like Trojans in the background.

Although you insist on remaining anonymous, we salute your efforts!

Contents

The Dummies' Guide to Serial Killing by Danuta Reah | 1

A Head for Heights by Shirley Golden | 15

Tatarabuela by Kester Robert Park | 23

Looking at the Wall by Mary Brown | 35

Car Park Girl by Josephine Greenland | 39

The School Run by Rebecca Perkin | 47

How to Wake a Dragon by Brittany Muscarella | 55

The Key by Carole Sleight | 63

F for Finality by Dean Moses | 71

Safe Passage by Laura Stump | 77

Princess Genevieve's Infinite Choices by Jenna Samuels | 85

Acts of Courage by Alan Paine | 93

Bioluminescence by Louisa Morillo | 101

The Beholder by Lauren Everdell | 105

Feta and Watermelon by Konstantina Sozou-Kyrkou | 113

Daughters of The Frost World by Ulla Susimetsä | 119

Foreword by Penny Grubb

When I was asked if I would write the foreword to this anthology, I hesitated. Although the theme of female strength appealed to me, I did have a sneaking concern that I might be presented with a worthy collection that preached women's rights at me. Don't get me wrong, I'm right behind the women's movement and equality for everyone, but when I settle down with a compilation of short stories, I'm not looking to have my consciousness raised, I'm looking to be entertained. Then I sampled the stories and knew it would be fine. I was gripped from the first word.

The history of women through the ages has seen many significant milestones, but even in the countries where women have the vote and legal equality with men, there is work to be done to achieve true equality; and it is sobering to be reminded that for most of the world's women their prospects are still limited by law.

Every major milestone for women has been hard-won and resulted from grassroots movements demanding change. And it looks as though the conception and creation of this anthology has tracked the emergence of a new wave of action in the move for equality for women, typified by the #MeToo movement that spread virally in October 2017. If you're curious why an independent publisher from the east coast of England should choose this moment to create a book to celebrate female strength, you're not alone. The word is that the CEO's team at Fantastic Books Publishing were inspired by the 'Rebel Girls' movement. Whatever the origins of the idea, they certainly caught the zeitgeist with this one.

The book captures the very essence of female strength, shown in ways that will captivate, surprise, shock and sometimes make you laugh aloud. It was not unexpected, given the history from which the current generation of writers have emerged, that the contenders for this anthology featured violence against women and abusive relationships as a repeated theme, but this was not the major theme. I was swept up into a sea of storytelling that took me from the modern world and present day to other worlds and times; I was gripped by tales told through fantasy, science-fiction, romance, the retelling of ancient fables, and unusual forms where I, as the reader, was the final arbiter of the outcome.

Enjoy the read!

July 2018

The Dummies' Guide to Serial Killing

Danuta Reah

The girl jogged up the path, her legs gleaming below the cut-off shorts. In the moonlight, her shadow danced between her feet as she ran through the gate and on to the road.

He'd watched her before. Within the hour, she would be back.

And tonight was the night.

The moon was shining through his bedroom window, cold and remote. He held the knife up so the pale light caught the blade. It was flat, it could almost be dull, but the edge glinted. The tip curved slightly upwards. The bolster – he'd been studying knives, so he knew what each part was called – fitted seamlessly into the handle which was wrapped with a leather thong to give the best grip.

It was a thing of beauty.

He lifted it in his hand – *hefted* it, that's what you did with a knife – trying to test the balance, but he wasn't sure what he was looking for. It didn't matter. It was a good knife. The balance would be right. He slipped it into the inside pocket of his jacket. His late mother's cat watched him from its place on the window-sill. It was thin and bedraggled. His mother used to spoil it, but he was teaching it a few hard lessons.

His breath quickened with excitement but he needed to be cool. He needed to keep his head.

The Dummies' Guide to Serial Killing says:

What is a serial killer? A true serial killer:
- *has at least three victims*
- *has a distinctive signature*
- *takes a 'cooling off' period which spaces out his killings.*

Even if you are tempted to try and find short cuts, multiple victims are not the way to go. A disaffected school student, or an employee with a grudge and a gun have not earned the title 'serial killer'. The true serial killer is an artist, and the true artist is passionate but painstaking. He cares. Remember: the soubriquet 'Zodiac' was not earned overnight!

The Dummies' Guide to Serial Killing says that successful serial killers are intelligent and well-informed, so he always looked up the words he didn't know like 'soubriquet', 'disaffected', and 'painstaking' He was a bit disappointed with the definition of painstaking. It had sounded more interesting than it actually was, but he mustn't let himself get bogged down in minor issues. He had to remain focused on the task.

And the task was now. Tonight. He had an hour to complete his preparations. He began his checklist.

1. The weapon.
The Dummies' Guide to Serial Killing said:

Your weapon is your true friend. You must know it and understand it, so when the time comes, it will do your bidding.

2

He took the knife out of his pocket and stood upright in front of the mirror, holding the blade over the palm of his left hand. That's what you did when you were going to make an oath. He'd seen it on TV. You drew the blade across your palm and then shared the blood. His blood would be on the knife when he … did all the things he planned to do. He would share his blood.

With her.

He admired himself in the mirror for a moment longer. The serial killer. Then he took a deep breath and drew the knife across the exposed flesh.

There was a clatter as the knife hit the floor. He doubled over, tucking his hand between his legs, his face screwed up. Shit. *Shit!* He hadn't expected it to hurt so much, he hadn't expected *his* knife, to hurt *him*. And despite the pain there wasn't much to see. The cut wasn't deep. It was a red line with a few beads of blood welling up.

He squeezed it, and the beads became a trickle that stopped as soon as he stopped squeezing. Still, blood was blood. He picked up the knife and returned it to his pocket.

Back to the checklist.

Weapon.

Tick.

2. Practice.

The Dummies' Guide said a lot about the importance of practising, of familiarising yourself with the rituals of killing.

Successful serial killers never flinch at the crucial point.

He was a bit upset at the accusation he might flinch, but in fact, the book – The Book – was right. The first cat – he'd done his first cat before he read The Book, and he had flinched. A bit. After a few more, he didn't flinch at all. His gaze moved to his mother's cat hunched on the window-sill. He'd been saving it up for the real thing.

Tonight.

For years, he'd been a dreamer, a pathetic wannabe who read about the heroes and tried to pretend he was one of them – one who hadn't actually started yet. But who would. Who had he thought he was kidding?

And then he found the book. He'd found it online, through one of his forums.

He spent a lot of time on forums. There was the one about his heroes, the greatest serial killers. That was good. And the one about The Manson Family – they weren't true serial killers, he realised that now. But they were cool, everyone agreed they were cool.

And then he'd found the Meet-Up space, *Dying for a Chat*.

That was pretty hardcore – or so he'd thought. At first. You had to be invited, and there was security and passwords and different levels. After he found it and got accepted, he'd spent night after night on the site, talking and sharing, stories and images – oh, the images – until the small hours. He'd really believed, then, that they were people like him, people who under-stood. He'd called himself Killer, and they had names like Candyman and Hunter.

But after a while, it wasn't enough anymore. Everyone talked a lot, everyone had stories, but no one really did anything. One of them, who called himself Cannibal, actually said how he'd eaten someone's liver with what he called *favour* beans and *a nice Chianti*, and another had an icon that made the *fefefefe* noise. Cannibal probably thought that fava beans was just another name for Heinz. And that Chianti was a kind of lager.

He'd looked up fava beans – and Chianti – later that night.

He was learning. *He* was improving himself.

Gradually he'd come to understand that none of these people were the real deal, but he'd hung around anyway. There was nothing else. Until the day he posted about the cat. His first cat. Some of them had actually criticised him. Criticised. Him. *That's not cool, Killer*, Candyman said. Cannibal actually blocked him.

Pathetic.

He almost gave up on the forum then, but the cat post was the one that did it. Shortly after, he saw the private message box flashing at the bottom right of his screen. That was interesting in itself because he hadn't turned messaging on. But there it was.

It was from someone called Karma. Karma used an icon like two tombstones, which was cool, and the message was short and to the point: *Killer. Your name is tragic. Check out this link.*

At first, it made him angry. His name was *tragic*, was it? What kind of stupid name was *Karma*? Some kind of sex book, wasn't it? A bit of politeness wouldn't have hurt. It didn't cost anything.

But real serial killers weren't polite. And somehow Karma had bypassed all the site security to make contact.

That was cool. So he clicked on the link.

At first, it looked like a bust. Karma, whoever he was with his pathetic name, was making fun of him. It was a site selling honey, of all things. Expensive jars of honey.

But later the same day, Karma got in touch again. *Before you sign up, read the Terms and Conditions carefully. Very carefully.* So he did, pages of them until he found the secret link. And that …

That *was* the real thing.

There were pictures. Videos. Sound files.

He spent a long time with those, especially the videos.

And that was where he found the link to The Book. *The Dummies' Guide to Serial Killing.* At first, he was angry. It was like the writer was making fun of him. *Dummies' Guide.* But that was just camouflage. The Book explained it. Serial killers need to wear camouflage – not really, he understood once he'd read a bit more. Serial killers had to hide in the crowd, make themselves the same as the crowd. That was what camouflage meant. It was a pity because the clothes were cool and had been quite expensive, but he trusted The Book now.

The Book told him who he was and what he had to do.

And now it was almost time …

He needed to finish his checklist. Practise.

A few stray cats, his oath – he knew he wasn't going to flinch. Practice. *Tick*.

3. Choosing the right name.

The Dummies' Guide to Serial Killing was very clear about the importance of a good name:

A successful serial killer will select a name with the same care he works out his modus operandi. (Modus operandi means the way you work. He'd looked it up.)

The name must be memorable. If you don't get this right, the reporters might name you themselves (and remember: all successful serial killers get on the news) or even worse, they may not name you at all.

Tip: you can make a name memorable by choosing certain features. A name can:
- *Rhyme: everyone remembers Hannibal the Cannibal*
- *Alliterate: Darkly Dreaming Dexter and Buffalo Bill are hard to forget*
- *Inform: The Collector, Jack the Ripper. These names make it clear exactly what this serial killer does*
- *Describe: Bluebeard. These names describe a physical attribute of the killer and create fear.*

Without a name, a serial killer is just another murderer.

He'd never heard of Bluebeard. It sounded a bit sad to him, but when he looked it up, he saw that Bluebeard was one of the best. Ever. Still, these days you couldn't go round with your beard dyed blue. He didn't even have a beard, for that matter.

He liked The Collector, but his *modus operandi* couldn't involve collecting. His flat was too small. A physical attribute? He looked at himself in the mirror. He didn't really have any, or not any good ones. Maybe he should have got a tattoo – a discrete one of course. Only a stupid serial killer would get tattooed on the face, though he kind of liked the thought.

She would look at him, and he'd draw his scarf back and she'd see the tattoo and know who he was. She'd scream then, but of course, it would be too late …

What about The Slayer …

Or The Gutter …

Great. He had almost named himself after a bit of roof. He hit the table with his fist in frustration. If he wasn't careful, he'd end up making a fool of himself. Tonight was the night and he didn't have a name. He'd got the weapon, he'd done the practice but he still didn't know what he was going to call himself!

Choosing a name … He couldn't tick that box yet.

OK. Moving on.

4. Choosing your first victim

The Dummies' Guide to Serial Killing said:

> *Great care must be taken over victim selection, especially your first victim. You will make most of your mistakes with her.*
>
> *Tip: don't choose someone you know well. Remember that's how they caught Buffalo Bill!*

He was right on top of this. Or – he wished he'd get a chance to say this out loud, or at least say it on the right forum – *she* was right on top of *him*. He'd done his research. It was *serendipity* (another word The Book had taught him). She'd moved into the upstairs flat a couple of weeks ago, but he didn't know her. They'd never spoken.

She went out each morning, presumably to work, and each evening, she came running down the stairs in those tiny shorts that showed off all her legs, and her … things … joggling about under her T-shirt.

Dumb cow.

And when she came home from her run, about an hour later – he knew because he spent a lot of time watching her – she didn't come back through the front gate where the road was and all the people going past. No, she came through the back gate that led into the small yard and went into the flats through the basement entrance.

The basement entrance was dark and hidden. No one else used it.

In the basement, there was just a storage cupboard for each flat and steps that ran up into the main building. If the door at the top of the steps was locked, then anyone who went into the basement was trapped.

Like a fly, in the web *he* had created.

Choosing your first victim. *Tick.*

He looked at his watch. Twenty minutes to go. It was time for the cat. First the cat, and then the dumb cow. That was his way. The cat was still watching him from the windowsill. He picked up his knife and reached over the pile of comics on top of the shelf to grab it by the scruff.

The cat arched and spat. Its paw moved fast and a sharp pain stabbed into the back of his hand. The knife dropped to the floor with a clatter. There was a hiss, and the cat was on top of the wardrobe.

He sucked the blood off his hand, angry now. The cat was going to learn a hard lesson. It had hurt him, and you didn't get away with that. You didn't hurt–

Of course. *The Cat*. That was it. That was his name. That was his signature – the dumb cow and the cat, together. His check list was complete.

Choosing a name. *Tick*.

Oh, he was going to have fun now. He pulled the chair across the room and stood on it, reaching towards the animal who backed away, still hissing, almost like it knew. He grabbed at it again but it twisted away, bit him and leapt over his shoulder on to the floor. The chair teetered and he jumped off, making the room shake. The bedroom door sprung open and the cat fled. He swore, sucking the blood from his hand where the cat had bitten him.

The cat was going to spoil it all.

But then he realised it didn't matter. It couldn't escape from the flat. It would be hiding, but he'd find it. He could do it later.

Afterwards.

Now it was time to get ready. He shook out the dark blue coverall and pulled it on, standing in front of the mirror to check the effect. In his pocket he had his knife and what The Book called the serial killer's best friend, a roll of duct tape.

5. Modus Operandi

He knew exactly what he was going to do. She'd come through the back gate, go to the basement entrance. The basement light would be on – she wouldn't go in if there was no light – but it would be dim because he'd changed the bulb. She wouldn't see him standing in the shadows by the door. She'd go up the steps leading into the flats, turn the handle of the door at the top.

Which would be locked.

Should he come up the stairs behind her? Even say, 'Good evening'?

Or should he be waiting for her at the bottom?

The Dummies' Guide to Serial Killing said:

plan well but be flexible. Always be prepared for the unexpected and adapt your plans accordingly. Tip: measure twice, cut once!

And then – he could take his time. Thanks to the duct tape, he could take all the time he wanted.

He stared out of the window, thinking about it, then he shook himself back into the here and now. Don't waste time dreaming. It's going to happen. It's going to be real.

Soon, he told himself.

Soon.

And afterwards he would leave her there. They'd find her quickly enough. He'd go back to his flat and grab the cat – he'd have to do it fast, but it wouldn't matter, not after what he'd just done.

Should he go back into the basement so he could leave the cat beside her? No, that was too much of a risk. He'd leave the cat in the bushes outside. It wasn't perfect, but he was being flexible, like The Book said. *Measure twice, cut once.* Then he'd clean the knife and put it away. Until the next time. The coverall would go into a big padded envelope.

And tomorrow – this was genius – he was going to take the envelope down to the post office and send it to a made-up address in Glasgow. He'd have to get it weighed, have to talk to the woman behind the counter who always looked at him as if he smelt or something, but that didn't matter. By the time they found it – *if* they found it – she would have forgotten. Or it would be too late.

He knew quite a lot about her. She lived on her own. With her cat. Modus operandi. *Tick.*

Tick.

Tick.

And now he's waiting in the shadows by the door that leads into the basement. He feels as though he's been waiting a long time, but it's only been five minutes when he checks his watch.

He can hear her. She's approaching the basement, breathing hard, stumbling slightly as if she's more tired than she expected to be. She opens the door, and he can see her silhouetted against the moonlight. She doesn't see him in his cave of shadows.

Then she's past him, heading towards the steps up out of the basement, towards the locked door.

She's trapped. He's got her.

Moving silently, he follows her. Then something brushes past him and he freezes, his heart hammering.

Not now! Not when he's so ready.

But it's only the cat, running up the stairs behind her. It must have got out of the flat when he opened the door.

It doesn't matter. In fact, it's even better. If she heard anything – and she didn't he's sure of that – but if she did, she'll think it's the cat. And now he'll have the cat in here with him. Just like he planned. No one can stop him now.

The dumb cow. Dead.

The cat. Dead.

She's almost at the door now. He hangs back, wanting to hear what she does when she finds it's locked. Will she be scared? Will she realise?

He jumps as he hears her speak. He's never heard her voice before. 'Hello, puss. What are you doing down here? You hungry again? He doesn't look after you, does he?'

Oh, she'll pay for that. And he'll let her see how well he can look after a cat in a few minutes. Once the duct tape is in place he can take all the time in the world.

But she's not talking to the cat any more. She says something under her breath, sounding annoyed, a bit irritated, and she rattles the door. He can't let her do that. His heart is beating fast. It's now. Now! Quietly, quickly, he flies up the steps.

She hears him, and half turns, the cat in her arms, but he's right in front of her holding the knife towards her face.

'Shut up. I won't hurt you.'

She lets the cat fall from her hands and it flees.

Too late, cat. Too late.

But she ducks and slides, and suddenly she's under his arm and past him, running down the steps ahead of him.

Running towards the outer door.

He leaps down the steps behind her, momentum carrying him forward, and she's there, in front of him, kneeling, just the way it was supposed to be, only not, only not …

In his dreams, she wasn't the one holding the knife.

Karma watched the final twitches with clinical interest. This bit was always an anti-climax, frankly. Still, she was done here. It had been trickier than she'd expected. She thought he would attack as she came into the basement. She hadn't credited him with the intelligence to lock the door at the top of the steps. Oh well. You live, and you learn.

So much for planning.

The cat wound round her legs, purring. She picked it up. It was going to need a home. Well, she could do that. It was time to take a break after all, take – she smiled – her 'cool down' period.

Then she could go back to her site and wait for another one to walk into her honey trap.

The Dummies' Guide to Serial Killing, by Karma.
- *First find your dummy*
- *That's it.*

∽ the end ∽

ABOUT THE AUTHOR

Danuta Reah is an invited contributor to this collection. She holds an international CWA Short Story Dagger for *No Flies on Frank,* which was included in The Best British Mysteries IV anthology published by Allison & Busby in 2006. Danuta, who also writes under the name Carla Banks, is the author of seven crime novels, a novella, and many short stories. As well as her novels, Danuta is a respected academic writer whose work is widely recognised in the field of language study, and which covers topics as diverse as how the press creates monsters and how to address a thousand-year-old vengeance demon.

A Head for Heights

Shirley Golden

I dream of possibilities, stretching further than the rope. I wobble in the middle. It's a trick Velius taught me to capture the crowd. Even those who would like to see me fall, hold their breath as though submerged beneath the Tiber. I exhale a giant's sigh as I reach the other side. The ground rumbles with a thunder of staffs and boots, and I descend toward the platform.

But Velius does not look pleased. 'Too slow,' he hisses.

He'd like to see me sprint from end to end, dance upon the line like an immortal. He wants to show the world the power that he believes is his to control. His hooded eyelids give the impression he only half watches, but I know better.

'Out back.' He flicks a nail-gnawed thumb towards the exit, and my stomach knots in expectation. 'Be quick,' he says, as if I need reminding.

Rufus leans against the doorway. Murmillon fins are etched into his helmet. They reflect rays of sunlight and I blink. I can identify him, even from the topmost rows of the Colosseum – the only position from which women are allowed to watch – even at midday when the sun dazzles and burns my arms as I shield my eyes to see.

Behind Rufus, a line of his followers litter the path; they press to touch, to capture strength and luck. I worry they take a piece of him with each grasp, but he allows it and laughs. I draw him away from them. He pushes off his helmet and it thuds to the ground. He kisses me and I twist, vine-like, around him.

He calls me his Venus and says he adores me. But it is he whom the people love. He's worshiped with religious fervour, only Jupiter receives more praise. He's their image of speed and strength; their sculpture of perfection. I'm just a woman with a head for heights.

We sometimes stay in his room above the bakery. It's warm and scented, comforting, but for the risk of fire. Velius does not prevent my visits, but nor does he condone them – my association with an idol does his pocket no harm. If I'm late for my sunrise training sessions, he knows where to find me, no need to send sentries or dogs.

Rufus has received the *Rudis* – the wooden sword that represents freedom – from the Emperor, Domitian, a shrewd, hard man. I am sceptical of this gift, which seems as cheap as the splinters that roughen the sword's edge.

Rufus only fights on the most auspicious occasions. He says he needs the coin; I say he's wedded to accolade. He keeps an eye on our future and expects the sun will burn brighter every day.

'Soon I'll own your freedom,' he says, drawing me closer.

I smile and run my fingers along his chest, over muscle, skin and hair. It makes me uneasy when he names my freedom as a possession.

'I will buy you and we'll marry.'

I scrunch up my nose. He has said this before. I never consent because it is not a question. 'You think Velius will sell me?' I've seen the glint of his eyes when he collects coins for admission to my show. I think of the slaves who have tried to escape, the ones I've seen dragged back and beaten and not get up again.

'I will convince him,' Rufus says, assured of his power. 'And we can leave the city, buy land and be indebted to no one.'

I love to walk the line, to feel my way in balanced perfection, far above the lives of plebeians and patricians. If we marry, my debts will remain. I'll no longer tread this threaded path, no longer feel the thrill of the audience with their sucked-in silence. I'll swell with his seed and will grow into an ordinary woman. Why then would he love me above those who fling themselves at him like arrows in battle?

He sprawls across the bed, one arm thrown across my belly, like a chain around the midriff of a slave, and when I try to roll into my own space, his muscles tighten.

When he fights, it is always the same. We separate at a side gate to avoid the crowds. I need not pay an entry fee with sesterces, for I can slip past the guards, who know me by my own reputation. They wink as I pass.

'Wish me luck,' Rufus says, clamping my face in his weather-worn palms.

'Are my wishes so vital?'

'One hundred, one thousand women may say it, but it is your word I crave.'

I kiss my finger and place it on to his lips as if to quiet his fears. 'Luck,' I murmur.

He grins and the track-lines on his face deepen into valleys.

He'll re-enact his Gaul origins in the arena, fighting in the style he learnt as a boy, because that's what the people demand. For all else, he is forced to adopt Roman ways, but struggles with the nuances of their language. I was brought to these shores not so long ago from Actium; yet new expressions come to me as easily as my poise. When I offer to teach him, he shrugs and says, 'Words do not make a man great, only deeds are important.'

I think he will not be bested by a woman.

He's to fight a *Hoplomachus*. I think of those warriors with their heavy armour, fashioned from Greek soldiers, and I shudder.

Rufus laughs at my fears. 'After tomorrow,' he tells me, 'I'll have enough coin for your release.'

So, he takes my wishes and strides off content, though I've gifted him with that which I do not possess.

The afternoon is hot and crammed. The Emperor is no more than a vase height in the distance. He leans forward. His mouth gapes like a trout, drowning in air, only this is no helpless gesture. Sometimes he indicates mercy but mostly he signs for death, and the crowd roars at the honour: death and glory! They do not distinguish between the two. Better than the shame of those too fearful to fight, the ones who stand mute in the centre while urine weeps down their thighs.

I dream of tying a rope above the arena and climbing closer to the gods. I'd balance beyond the blood-thirsty screams of the mob. I'd shut my eyes and imagine the rope motionless, untouched by the afternoon breeze. The people would fall silent, and the sun would be free to scorch every head. No shelter. No status.

Rufus strolls into the ring. He's smaller than the Emperor from here. He raises his fist and the crowd roars. The *Hoplomachus* trots from the gates, wearing his armour with ease; he sets his bronze shield in a spin, and I hold my breath. I press both hands firmly against my belly.

Rufus and his opponent face the Emperor and salute. A deathlike hush descends as each man circles the other. The *Hoplomachus* raises his arm, lance poised. I swallow, thick and dry.

I want to turn away but find I can't. Around me are cries of impatience, cries of support, and cries for blood, even before the first blow has been struck. I catch the trace of sweat, not quite masked by the rose petal beads strung around wrists and necks. I imagine the white-knuckled hold the *Hoplomachus* has on his lance, but from this distance the details are lost.

Rufus slashes his long sword towards his rival's underarm. The *Hoplomachus* sidesteps, twisting and thrusting his lance towards Rufus' thigh. The man in front of me roars and flings his arms skyward, blocking my view. I half stand. Rufus holds his shield high, his blade ready to strike. I clamp a hand over my mouth.

The *Hoplomachus* jabs his spear, and Rufus thrusts his sword. The spear cracks into two pieces, the broken ends are jagged and pale. Rufus breaks from the cover of his shield. The *Hoplomachus* swivels, dodges the blade. He rotates his weapon to amuse the crowd, flamboyant and confident. His dagger is a fang: smooth, sharp and hungry.

As it eats into Rufus' side, both seem surprised. Rufus glances upwards, perhaps searching for me. He staggers and falls. A dark patch creeps across his midriff, and spreads like muddy water on to sand.

My vision fogs and my world blurs. The crowd's excitement falls to a murmur. My heart aches with each beat. I clench and unclench my hands beneath the folds of my stola. We wait for the Emperor's verdict. Domitian thinks defeat is worse than death and no doubt Rufus does too. So, the Emperor gives his variety of mercy and my future husband turns from a possibility to nothing in the time it takes to signal dismissal with an imperial flick of the hand.

My tears are a speck of dust in the ash of Mount Vesuvius. I hear the cries and sobs of his followers and scattered cheers from those who backed the other man. The jangle and exchange of coins has never sounded so brutal. I am Atlas, the weight of the world hard upon my shoulders.

Below, a figure runs into the arena: it is Velius. He bows before the Emperor and waits for a different sign.

'Come,' Velius bellows. 'Would you mourn the passing of a hero? We must not shed tears, but honour his noble memory.' He signals, impatient that I should approach. His slaves construct ladders and platforms; they fix the rope taut from one end to the other.

I walk across the arena to a chorus of cheers. Velius stands before me. His form blots out the sun. Behind him, slaves run to their task. They collect the body and cover weapons, flesh and bone.

'This is your moment, Natasa,' he tells me. 'Use it well.'

I can barely balance on solid ground. I shake my head. My gaze is drawn to the slaves, kicking sand over dark blood stains.

Velius' eyes widen. He prods my stomach, hard. 'You think I haven't noticed? In a few months you'll be no more use to me than an actor who's lost his tongue – a worthless, less than ordinary slave. If you want to stay, you'd better earn well now.' He shoves me towards the platform.

I rub my belly, the bulge is non-existent. Rufus never guessed.

My vision clears and I walk towards the platform, head held high, back straight. I climb, and never has the ascent felt so vast, as if it'll take me beyond reach, beyond control. Up on the wooden planks, I wait for the crowd to calm. I circle my belly with one hand. One step is easy enough, but another and another?

The line feels shaky beneath my feet but the way ahead is clear. I wobble in the middle, and the crowd suck a collective hissed intake of air.

I pause and look down upon them all. I can feel the growing vitality inside of me. She will be born strong and free. For her, I leap forth to sprint the last, and I'll dance upon the line like an immortal.

∼ the end ∼

ABOUT THE AUTHOR

Shirley Golden's work is published in various places in print and online; occasionally, she has won prizes for short fiction. She is part of an editorial team who select stories for the FlashFlood Journal, created in 2012 to help celebrate National Flash-Fiction Day.

Learn more about Shirley on her website: www.shirley-golden.net and follow her on Twitter: @shirl1001

A Head for Heights was one of the three major prize winning stories.

Tatarabuela

Kester Robert Park

On Thursday evenings, Tim pretended to be a girl. He screamed like a girl, ran like a girl, and fought like a girl. He marched across moors, sang war songs and raised the blood of his companions with war cries yelled into the icy vectors of snowstorms, all very much like a girl.

The girl in question, more properly a young woman, was called Katarina Emilia Corazón de León, crystal blue of iris, shapely of bust and thigh, leather clad and as a deadly as a knife. You can just see her now, with a hawk on her gauntleted wrist, hair swirling around her face, vengeful and intimidatingly sexy.

At that point, Norm had been Dungeon Master for several months, and had forced the urban adventurers out of their built-up, chunky sky-lined comfort zone and out into the greys and browns of the Savage Lands for, as Norm put it, some 'proper adventurin''. Tim, who was a friend of Leonard, had been allowed to join the group, and so their avatars in the Realm of Light and Dark had met Katarina on a mountain trail. She had explained that she was perfectly alright on her own thank you, but then the shadows of three ogres had darkened their hopes of an uneventful journey and, later, they had all agreed over a flagon of ogreish scragge that a bit of back-up was perhaps not to be sniffed at, after all.

Krodloth (played by Sid), Irielle (Leonard) and Frigg Friggsson (Charles) found that Katarina was kind to her friends, true to her God, and vicious to her enemies. They made speeches atop a portentous-looking tor by the wilderness trail and welcomed her warmly into the Fellowship of the Moist Flagstone.

'Should've been a wizard,' muttered Sid.

'Or a ranger,' mumbled Charles.

Neither Norm nor Leonard said anything. Tim's plump lips merely protruded further from his hairy face, and he wondered when he would eventually feel rejected enough to drop out of the group.

At the end of Tim's fourth session, they arrived at the mouth of a cavern wherein slept the scaly beast who had laid waste to the countryside some eighteen summers past. Irielle and Krodloth in particular had been raised amongst the burnt debris of that thoughtless terrorism.

Norm read from the curly scrawls in his notebook. 'At last you stand at the maw of dragon's lair. The blackness is penetrated … *shut up Sid* … by odd points of light which are suggestive of a corridor curving out of sight. As you draw closer, you feel a warm, humid breeze on which a subtle odour hangs, musky and rank, accompanied by the sweet sourness of excreta and rotting flesh.'

'Sounds a bit like Leonard's bedroom,' guffawed Charles.

'You would know, lover boy,' replied Leonard, winking.

'Well, before we get to the mum jokes, that's our cliffhanger for tonight,' announced Norm, 'but you'd better ready yourselves for a fear check, start of next sesh, and it looks a bit bleak for some of you.'

'Not Krodloth!' said Sid. 'Nothing scares Krodloth!'

Charles looked at Tim. 'You might just want to head to the pictures next week, Tim.'

'What? Why?'

'Irielle's immune to fear effects. Krodloth can use *Rage* and I … I mean, Frigg comes from generations of beastslayers, but your Xena the Warrior Princess, she's just a girl, better off out of it.'

Tim looked at Charles' face and saw he wasn't joking.

'I favour roleplay over rolling dice,' said Norm. 'If you can explain Xen–, um, Katarina's motivation for walking into this deathtrap, you won't have to roll.'

At eleven minutes past noon the next day, Tim caught his own skewed reflection in the glass door of The Roasted Bean. The word 'lank' pierced its way into his mind. He went in, jangling the little bell and sat down opposite a sofa littered with mobile office equipment; his friend Lucy operating fluidly within it all.

'Alright, *dude*,' she said, not looking up.

'Alright dude, yourself, *dude*,' he replied, occupying himself with the coffee menu.

'How's work?'

'Fine. Well, a bit annoying. I've been using my boss's e-mail account this week. Loads more clarifications than usual. Stupid questions about stuff that I've already covered.'

'Trish is your boss, right?'

'Yeah, that's her.'

'That's why, then.'

'What's why, then?'

'People are more likely to query stuff if a woman tells them. I was just reading about it in this journal.'

'That's insane.'

'As is life, young grasshopper.'

Lucy took off her glasses, shook the exotic colours of her hair away from her face and looked at him. She looked tired, but only if you looked at her eyes.

'I've been thinking.'

A three-word phrase more terrifying has never been uttered, Tim thought.

'Did it hurt?'

'I'll hurt you in a second. No, it's about the Youthie. We've got a bit of a gap.'

'What kind of gap?'

'We've got these new kids in at the moment and they're into, you know, computer stuff.'

'I see, said the blind man. Got any more of that awesome intel, Luce?'

'Oh, you know. It's like World of Spacecraft. Dungeons and Unicorns.'

'You're doing that on purpose.'

'Yeah. Yeah, I am, but only a bit. Jeanie knows even less, and if it isn't football, don't ask Todd.'

'So?'

'So. We're actually a bit short-handed this weekend and we need … a really amazing, generous, talented bloke who's really good at all that geeky stuff.'

'Can't think of anyone.'

'*Tiiimmm!*'

'Oh, alright then.'

Lucy launched herself across the table.

'Stop kissing me! No more duck face! Hey!'

On Friday night, Tim had a drink with his father.

'What are you up to this weekend?'

'Not much. Oh, I got co-opted into Lucy's youth club.'

'Oh, that sounds fun.'

'Yeah, maybe.'

'I see what you mean. A good vibe can be tricky to keep up.'

'Lucy makes them hand in any sugary foods before they come in. She's fed up of peeling them off the ceiling.'

'Ah yes, the high-sugar diet of the modern child. Another big factor is the balance of girls and boys.'

'As in: too many boys and it basically turns into an indoor football club?'

'More or less … Listen, did I ever tell you about the time I volunteered in Ecuador with VSO?'

Only about a thousand times.

'Possibly, Dad.'

'I worked at a village school. As you went through the school from *basico uno* to the end of *colegio*, there were progressively fewer girls in the school.'

'Oh, why was that?' asked Tim.

'Well, I don't know, but I don't think girls' education was much valued. I assumed they were kept at home to help with chores, or maybe they got pregnant and dropped out.'

'Doesn't seem fair,' said Tim. 'What if they wanted to get out of that little village?'

'Exactly. And the other thing, in the classes that had no girls in them at all, the boys were little savages, impossible to teach anything, but the ones that had equal boys and girls were wonderful to teach. Lovely, respectful kids.'

And Tim listened, and thought.

On Saturday evening at about six, Tim finally emerged from the warmth of his flat. He was going to be late. On the way up Sand Street, he noticed a group of young women making their way up to the clubs, bare-legged right up to the thigh. Strappy dresses. Tim shivered. It was February.

And who gets called the strong sex? he asked himself.

Ten minutes later, he stood across the road from the Baptist Union Hall. The sounds of a football reverberating, the odd screech of mobile equipment, sudden yells and their echoes reminded him of a childhood which didn't seem so distant.

As he entered, Lucy was in the process of explaining something to a boy nervously trying to memorise her instructions, but she turned to wave. A girl with ribbons in her hair stuck her head around the double doors into the main hall, before slipping back inside.

'Theodore, there's a man here. Do you think he wants to be in our peace march? He's a really big man. Let's ask him.'

Duly, the girl emerged, leading Theodore by the hand.

'I'm Gemma and this is Theodore. He's only four. Do you want to help us with our peace march? We're organising it to stop wars in far away countries like Middle East and Texas.'

'That sounds like a brilliant idea. What's the plan?'

'Well, we're just going to march around the hall and I'm going to shout 'Stop War' every thirty seconds. Isn't that right, Theodore?'

'Okay, maybe we need a banner.'

'Yeah! Let's make a banner. Can I be in charge of the pictures?'

'I don't see why not,' he replied.

Tim was amazed by how quickly he had been drawn into something he actually liked, something that wasn't football. In fairness, it wasn't 'World of Spacecraft' either but it was exceptionally detailed fun and he supposed that that was what Lucy had meant by 'a gap'. Not only had the project inspired a gentle sense of hope in him, it seemed that their small project had functioned as patient zero in a small epidemic of peace poster-making now breaking out around the hall. He heard Lucy reminding some children to put the lids back on their pens, and went over to speak to her.

'Well, you've geeked the place right up,' she said. 'There's at least one dinosaur and about half a dozen robots.'

'I haven't even spoken to those kids.'

'Your geeky aura must've reached them.'

'Aw, that's not fair. I had a shower before I came out.'

She laughed, and smiled at him. He felt special, connected, part of the human race, and yet troubled.

'Did I tell you what happened at roleplaying last week?'

'You did not.'

He told her about Katarina Emilia and the medieval sex politics that was holding back her career as a dragonslayer.

'Fascinating,' she said. 'Man experiences male chauvinism. Well, it seems you have two choices: let it pass, or do something about it.'

'I want to do something. It's not fair on her! Even though she is me, it's like, she deserves to grow.'

'Everyone does.'

'Right.'

'Well, here's a thought that helps me from time to time. When you look at it, the world isn't divided into those who actively take opportunities away and those who have them taken. There's a horde of people in between who aren't one thing or the other. When those people take action, they're on the side of the underdogs, but when they do nothing, they're not neutral.'

'They're on the side of the status quo.'

'Exactly.'

'It doesn't seem like I have a choice at all, then.'

Lucy pressed her lips together and frowned.

'Let me know how you get on.'

Monday lunchtime, Tim got an unexpected phone call at work from his mum. He clicked the button on the portal to stop any urgent work coming through, and set it for half an hour.

'I can't believe it's been a whole year,' she said, after ten minutes of describing the new church minister (good voice but a bit too repetitive).

'Flown, hasn't it, since we were, you know …'

'Saying goodbye.'

Tim let the silence expand, unsure that any words of his could be at home in it.

'Your gran was one of nine you know. And *her* mum had them all without any anaesthetics.'

'Gosh, it wasn't that long ago, was it?'

'No, no. Your grandma was born in 1922.'

'Hang on. You're not telling me they didn't have anaesthetics for childbirth in the 20s.'

'Of course they did. No, your great grandparents – well, no, tell you the truth, it was your grandfather who distrusted basically all the new drugs and medicines coming out at that time, and told the doctors that your great grandmother wasn't to use them.'

'Good God!'

'Mind you, he changed his mind thirty years later, when he was dying of pulmonary asbestosis.'

'Eugh,' said Tim, but it made him think.

On Wednesday evening, Tim opened up the word processor on his computer and started to write. Two hours later, when it was much too late to get a decent night's sleep, he was printing out what he'd written.

He looked at it, rubbed his eyes and yawned with satisfaction.

On Thursday, just after his shift finished, he looked in the mirror in the toilet and wondered if he was really going to do this. It would be so easy to just give it a miss. He was tired anyway, and sure they'd understand. But then he tried to imagine himself explaining it to Lucy, and found that he didn't want to be there in that imaginary conversation, trying to justify why he'd hidden from something he knew was wrong. Disappointed imaginary-Lucy's expression was breaking his heart.

Half an hour later, he was pressing the buzzer for Norm's flat. The door clicked open without a word, and when he got up there, the front door was ajar. He entered to grunts of greeting.

Some half an hour later, they were all seated around the table. Tim had the printed piece of paper in his hand, folded into eighths.

Norm opened his notepad and reminded them that the party was standing at the cavern mouth and suffering the particular odours of the dragon's lair.

'I utter a prayer to Aroweth, for courage in battle,' declared Leonard.

'Aroweth looks down on Irielle and blesses him with the bravery to proceed,' agreed Norm.

'Krodloth thinks about all the family members that got burnt to death by this abomination and goes berserk with rage,' says Sid.

'Sorry, Sid. Berserkers still have to make fear checks.'

'Shit.'

The sound of angular plastic rolling across wood.

'17 total.'

'You fail the check–'

'What!?'

'I set the difficulty at 20.'

'That's ridiculous!' Sid smirked in his rage. 'Well, I s'pose I'll just have to pass the time with the lovely Katarina while you blokes are getting your heads ripped off.'

'Well …' started Tim. Curiosity gently flowed in his direction.

'My character has something to say.'

'Go on then,' said Norm.

Nervously, Tim unfolded his piece of paper.

'She puts her hands on her hips and says, "You men … in the silence before battle, you would have us believe that all your thoughts are of God and glory, but I know … I have fought with men before, more honest and brave than you. We fought our way into enemy mountains and after months of living on the edge of fear and starvation, there was but one thought on their minds. Perhaps their lover, or their mother, or their sister, but always a woman. The one man whose whole family had been massacred was gone insane, just a murdering machine.

"You talk to me as if I am fit for collecting flowers but the truth is that without the women in your life, your desperation would turn in on you, and eat … you … alive.

"My grandmother gave birth to nine children, on each occasion, with just one girl attending to her; and hot water and clean cloths. According to the tale, she did not cry or scream once as she bore life after life into this world. Did your fathers scream when they were cut or scorched …? You don't need to answer.

"Men, we will enter this cavern. This dragon may be a fearsome creature, but she and I are connected. She is my *tatarabuela*, my great grandmother. Yes, I have the blood of dragons in my veins. All women do. And let me tell you this. I haven't come here to slaughter and wreak revenge. I have come here to meet her. It is time for us to negotiate, woman to woman: warrior to warrior, to seek amity, so that all warriors, and their men and children may live in peace."'

The sound of papers rubbing together, of jeans against seat.

'Okay,' said Norm, voice hoarse. 'I suppose you'd better go in.'

∼ the end ∼

ABOUT THE AUTHOR

Kester Park is a prize-winning short-story author. He acquired an honours degree in Creative Writing from the University of Hull in 2009. Thereafter he passed into a phase of extended disorientation, possibly due to a spider bite.

When he became lucid, it was 2014, and he was half way up Mount Pichincha, in Ecuador, swathed in white robes, and faithful acolytes were writing down his every eructation on sacred parchments.

He is very content there as long as the yucca bread isn't too dry and someone wipes away the spittle once in a while.

Tatarabuela was shortlisted and highly commended by the judges.

Looking at the Wall

Mary Brown

They say, 'She just sits there, looking at the wall.'

Then they ask all these trivial questions: what day of the week is it? That doesn't matter. If you're retired and don't go to church, all days are alike; or rather each day is unique, individual, never to return. The day the Lord made for me to rejoice in.

What's the time? That doesn't matter either. If you live alone you eat when you're hungry, sleep when you're tired. I 'live in the moment,' as they say. Do they know what they mean by that? They can't; they haven't lived long enough. I understand: time doesn't matter to those who have arrived.

They don't ask the important questions: what are the stars singing tonight? Can you hear the seeds sprouting? I could answer those. I could tell them what the birdsong feels like, or how to touch the silence of dawn, or taste the peace of beauty. Can they hear the sap rising? This is what matters, not the day, the time, or even where the wars are.

I know the season. Ask me about spring greening and I can tell you all there is to know. What does it matter if it's Monday or Friday? The woods are a little greener than they were yesterday, not as green as they will be tomorrow. I can feel the green rushing headlong, as it puts an end to winter. That's what matters. That's life. I'm becoming part of it, in a way they can't; they haven't lived long enough. I understand, converse with, the powers of life.

They talk of putting me in a 'Home'. I will be at home wherever they put me. I once made a home for husband and children. Hard, unforgiving work: cooking, cleaning, tidying, thinking these things mattered. Now I know they do not.

'Mother, please,' they say now, as they carry dirty dishes to the sink and bang them around. When did I become Mother? Once I was Mummy. I liked that. Mummy knew what they needed. Then I became Mum, as the ties that bind gradually loosened. For years I cared for and protected them. Now they care, or think they care, for Mother; think they know what I need, as once I knew their needs.

Do they interpret my silences as subversion? Mute aggression perhaps, or the silence of senility? I live in the silence of eternity: a silence within me, which nurtures and sustains me. There is more to life than they dream of. More than cleanliness, tidiness. Otherwise what is there?

They say, 'She just sits there looking at the wall.'

Yes. I have time now to look and see, really see, what a wall is. It holds all life: all that is. I see love in a grandchild's sticky finger mark: love, the cement that holds the world together, that holds chaos at bay. I see a work of art in peeling paint; hear the gentle music of a spider's web. Out of doors walls teem with life: tiny cushions of brilliant green moss sparkle; diamonds glitter in grey stone; a mysterious blue haze lights up the mortar, with dark secrets. All life is there: all earth's history set in stone, waiting for me to take my place.

I can see all there is when I look at the wall. It is so simple. Why do they have to make it complicated?

I know what matters. Not the day or the month. I know who

I am, and where I'm going. The walls of a Home may be cleaner, but they won't be lifeless. I will seek out the mystery and the magic of life as long as I can breathe. Life is more real to me now than ever, precious as never before. I am learning from it, learning to be part of it, to enter its vast, lovely and loving spirit. Soon I shall be one with it, part of all that is. Until that time comes I shall continue looking at the wall.

$\sim$ the end $\sim$

ABOUT THE AUTHOR

Mary Brown is an invited contributor to this collection. She is a retired teacher and prison chaplain who saw prison from the other side of the bars when she spent ten days in HM Prison Holloway following her arrest at a peace protest in 1960. Mary wrote several non-fiction books during her working life, but had long nurtured an idea for a novel which she wrote and saw published following her retirement. Her debut novel, *I Used to Be,* was published to critical acclaim in 2017. Like much of Mary's writing, it focuses on those at the margins of society.

Car Park Girl

Josephine Greenland

Mum named me after a lettuce. Rapunzel leaves are heart-shaped and vivid green, easy to mistake for spinach. Mum got a craving for them when she was pregnant with me. She sent Dad over to Granny's every morning to fetch some for her.

Granny told me rumours spread through the neighbourhood about the name Mum had chosen for me. People glanced at her as she passed down the street, quieted when she walked in upon a conversation. New age, they called her, and wrinkled their noses as if the word smelled bad.

They were right, I think. Here I am in the car park, perhaps one of the last of the human race, looking at the empty apartments shrouded by the dusty moon, Granny's head in my lap. A single Rapunzel in a concrete garden, suspended above the road.

When the bomb fell on the nuclear reactors and the radioactive waves soared through the air, the lettuce was seared to stumps. Along with the rest of the neighbourhood, the rest of the entire city, we scrambled into our car, cramming as many suitcases as we could into the boot and between the seats. I brought my violin too, despite Mum's protests. She would have made me leave it by the porch if Granny hadn't intervened.

We drove for three days. When the engine ran dry, we walked. We came to another husk of a city and took shelter in a multi-story car park. Mum and Dad closed and locked the garage door on the ground floor.

Mum cut my hair and wove it into a rope.

She assigned us rules: 'Rapunzel, you sweep the floor and cook. Granny, you manage the rationing and tend the fire. Dad and I will forage.' She looked at me. 'Oh, and Rapunzel, draw a calendar on the wall with the knife. It's important to keep count of the days.'

They took it in turns to climb down the wall using my rope. When they returned they called: 'Rapunzel, Rapunzel, let down your long hair.' And I lowered the rope to let them back up.

Radiation runs fast, it does not need a rope to climb walls. On our second morning at the park we woke to find rashes on our arms, which peeled when we scratched them. We vomited yellow ooze. Fever clutched us in the night, nausea hovered over us in the morning, migraines crept upon us during the day.

'We're dying, Mum,' I said and pulled at my hair. A tuft came out in my hands. 'Look. I'll be bald in a week.' I looked at Dad curled on the floor, at Granny, huddled over the fire and poking a stick into the flames. As we watched, she broke into a coughing fit so violent I thought she'd cough her lungs up. 'If I lose my hair, we're dead.'

'You're not … going down there.' Mum fixed me with a dead stare. 'You're the last Rapunzel. I won't let you get hurt.'

'By what?' I looked towards the apartments. 'Is it those people–?'

I walked to the edge. I heard Mum's footsteps behind me, then her hand closed over my mouth. Sweat and dirt stuck to my lips. I wanted to spit, but Mum's eyes compelled me to stay still. We were only a few steps away from the edge. I followed her gaze towards the point where the road took a turning around one of the apartments.

Four figures no bigger than matchsticks, two leaning against the wall, two standing in the road. They looked straight at us.

Mum guided us back to the middle of the car park, away from the edge. She let her hand fall. 'I saw them on the road,' she whispered. 'They grabbed someone – a girl, just your age.' She gripped me by the arms. 'Rapunzel, if they come wandering here when I'm not around, don't let them up.'

'Mum, are you sure–'

'They're soulless people, Rapunzel. They will cut open your stomach and eat your liver raw before you have a chance to scream.'

I looked into her bloodshot eyes. In the shade of the car park her pupils were black holes, so large they swallowed her irises.

'Ok,' I said.

I heard them the following day. Mum was foraging. I sat by the edge, playing an old bluegrass tune on my violin. The rope lay coiled in a pile beside me. Weedy voices trailed up the wall:

'Rapunzel, Rapunzel, let down your long hair.'

They were right below me. Four men, in leather jackets and torn jeans. All I could see of their hooded faces were their teeth, blackened and crooked.

I kept on playing. Their voices subsided beneath the notes, blurred beneath the sawing movements of the bow. The tune sped up, I slammed my clammy fingers against the board, saw the rosin rise like vapour from the strings.

The A string snapped with a twang. It coiled back to the conch, leaving a ghost line on the board. The voices quieted. The teeth leered at me. With the music gone, the distance between us vanished. The teeth were right beneath me, ready to wrench my feet from my ankles.

I crawled back to the wall in the middle of the parking space, violin clutched to my chest, and cowered on the ground until their voices faded.

The other strings went during the next couple of days. Even metal seemed to be no match for the radiation. 'It could make us a fire for two days,' Mum said.

'Don't even think about it,' Granny hissed. 'Isn't it enough trauma for her to sit trapped here all day without you chopping up her most precious item?'

Mum kicked a pebble lying in the ashes. She watched it scuttle across the parking space and hit the opposite wall. 'Its strings are breaking and she has no spares.'

One morning, I woke to find the case gone. Mum sat by the fire, tossing bits of the violin frame into the fire. There had been one string left.

I rose and approached, fists clenched.

When I reached her, I saw red rims circle her eyes. A tear oozed down her cheek. She looked up at me and shook her head.

The angry cry amassing in my throat melted away. I returned to my space, and never mentioned the violin again.

The following night, the men came back. They kicked at the door, pounded at the barred windows. Mum put an arm round me and pulled me close. 'Let them try,' she muttered in my ear. 'As long as I'm alive, they'll never get within a metre of you.'

I felt her hand press something into mine. It was the last violin string. I placed it in my coat pocket and burrowed my head against her chest. Her lips brushed over my hair.

She went foraging in the morning. 'Don't expect me back until the evening,' she told me.

Evening came and she was nowhere to be seen. I waited by the pillar for two days. On the third, I wrote an "M" in the calendar. It was our twenty-fifth day in the car park.

Granny introduced new sanctions on the rationing. 'One bite o' Mars Bar, one fist o' beans, one fist o' corn and one swig o' Lucozade. That's all you're having in a day, Rapunzel. Scrimp and save will see us to the end.' Her chestnut eyes beamed down at me on either side of her hawk shaped nose, daring me to question her.

She made her way over to Dad. 'Help us. Help us find more food. We're running out.'

Dad grimaced and covered his eyes. Now his head was naked and pristine like an egg. The rashes on his arms became blotches. They gouged into his flesh, leaving big cavities in the skin as if an animal had ripped out a part of him, but not bothered to finish him off.

'Daddy.' I bent over him, cradling his head in my lap. Tears dripped down my cheeks and hit him on the eyelids. One snuck in beneath his withered lashes. He drew in a deep, rattled breath. His head grew heavy and I realized that he was gone.

We carried him to the opposite corner of the parking space and covered his body with his jacket.

I did not draw a "D" in the calendar that day.

Granny continued with the rationing. 'Scrimp and save, Rapunzel, scrimp and save.' She scurried back and forth across the car space sweeping the floor with her jacket, tended to the fire, prepared our meals. Then she sheathed back into herself like the blade of a penknife and curled up in my lap.

Her hand fluttered to my knee. 'The knife, I've sharpened it.' She pressed a small object into my hand. 'Use it well,' she whispered.

She passed away just before the voices began again. I was relieved she couldn't hear them.

Sunlight pushes its finger through the night time mesh. Grey dresses grey as the light sweeps over the parking space and turns the dusty air to glitter.

Carefully, I lift Granny's head off my knees and stand. I avoid looking at her as I stomp out the fire and pack the rations in Dad's old rucksack. I take out the knife. *Use it well.* Spider web words, weaving their way through my mind.

'Is this what you meant, Granny?' I say and cut my hair. It only adds five inches to the rope.

I tie the rope round the pillar and lean into the air. Dust stings my eyes, and I have no more tears left to drive it away. The dust is a skin on my face, blinding me as I map my way down the wall.

My feet hit something hard. I blink the dust out of my eyes and see asphalt. It's quiet. Not a single voice, or thud of feet kicking metal.

I scan ahead one last time. 'Time to go,' I whisper, and stumble down the road, the nutty scent of Rapunzel ripe on my lips.

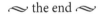 the end

ABOUT THE AUTHOR

Josephine Greenland has a BA in English from the University of Exeter and is currently studying for her MA in Creative Writing at the University of Birmingham. She has been published in Dream Catcher Magazine and shortlisted in competitions by TSS Publishing and Cinnamon Press. She is originally from Sweden.

Car Park Girl was awarded first prize in the competition.

The School Run

Rebecca Perkin

'Come on kids, we're going to be late!' Rachel said. She stood at the bottom of the stairs, her usual 8.20 a.m. spot. There were screams and shouts coming from above, but she didn't need to go up and see what was going on. She could picture it clearly: Claire, her youngest, would be standing half dressed with her socks in her hand and Joe, her brother, opposing her in nothing but his pants. They would be arguing over something trivial, like who could get dressed the quickest, or who had hidden the other's school uniform.

'You'll be late, again,' thirteen-year-old Luke said as he traipsed down the stairs, dragging his rucksack behind him.

'We're *not* going to be late,' Rachel said, adding, 'shouldn't *you* be gone by now.'

Luke took an apple from the bowl on the sideboard in the hall and shoved it into his bag.

'You're taking me today, remember?' He motioned to the gym bag, hockey stick and guitar case that were waiting patiently by the front door.

Rachel sighed and groaned.

'Why do you have to do so many extra-curricular activities?'

Her son raised his eyebrows at her as he stuffed some school books into his bag.

'Wasn't Dad taking you today? Claire! Joe! Get down here!'

Luke opened the front door. 'He had to leave for work early. He told you last night.'

Rachel nodded a little forcefully, having no recollection. She remembered making dinner for Claire and her school friend, then having a glass of wine, before checking her email and discovering ten from her boss. Tom, her husband, must have mentioned it to her then, when she was engrossed in the computer. She cursed her out-spoken, immaculately dressed boss, who she was sure disrupted her home life on purpose.

'Muuum,' Claire whined as she came down the stairs. 'Why do *I* have to go to school and you don't?'

Rachel turned away and noticed a letter on the side that she'd been meaning to post for days.

'I've been to school, sweetie. Now I have to go to work, a much more tedious and boring place.'

Claire didn't reply but sat on the bottom step and began to put her shoes on. Joe followed her down, making aeroplane noises as he came. When he got to the third step from the bottom, he jumped and an explosive sound left his mouth.

'Okay, come on guys, we've *got* to get going.' Rachel picked up the letter as they hurried out the door.

'*Joe.* Will you stop making those noises,' Rachel said, looking at him in the rearview mirror.

Joe exhaled hard, causing his thick lips to judder, then continued playing with his action figure. It was one that came with a missile and Rachel was forever finding pellets around the house and in the car. She'd even found some in her sandwich once at work, when some had shot their way into her handbag.

'I'll drop you off first,' Rachel said to Luke, who was busy texting.

As Rachel swung the car round a corner, Luke's guitar case flew from the passenger side, whacking her in the eye.

'Jesus Christ!' She shoved it back over to her son's side.

'Mummy swore!' Claire sung. 'Mummy swore! Mummy swore!'

'I asked you to put all that stuff in the boot.'

Luke didn't look up from his phone, but held on to the guitar case.

'Then I'd have to get it all out when we got there.'

Rachel rubbed her eye, checking it in the mirror when she stopped at a light. She could already see a bruise coming.

'Mummy why haven't you got shoes on?' Claire asked as she poked her head between the front seats.

Rachel looked down at her socks. She'd thought something had felt a little odd.

'See what you kids are doing to me,' she said. 'Good job I keep a spare pair in the boot.'

Fifteen minutes and a whole chorus of Little Mix's 'Black Magic' from Claire later, and Rachel pulled up outside Luke's school.

'I'll see you at half five,' Rachel said to Luke out her window as he stood by the car, trying to juggle all his stuff.

'Luke, heads up!' a voice called.

Rachel barely had time to look away from Luke when the hockey puck hurtled towards the car, whipping its way through the half wound down window and smacking her right in the mouth. She heard the crack, then tasted the blood and brought her hand to her mouth just in time to catch her tooth.

'Oh shit!' a voice said from outside.

'That's my mum, you dickhead,' Luke said, whacking his mate on the arm.

'Mrs Nelson, I'm so sorry. I've got terrible aim.'

Luke's friend stuck his spotty face through the car window.

In the back Claire began to cry.

'It's fine,' Rachel slurred, grappling in the glove compartment for some tissues. 'I needed a trip to the dentist anyway.'

It took ten minutes and a whole pack of travel tissues wedged in her gums, for the bleeding to stop. Rachel had wrapped her tooth in one of the tissues and stuffed it into her jacket pocket.

'Just keep quiet for a minute, you two,' Rachel said as she called her boss.

She explained she was going to be late and ignored the rant that bellowed at her down the phone. A few minutes later she hung up. She checked her face in the mirror and realised she looked like she'd been in a fight.

'Mummy, will you get money from the tooth fairy?' Claire asked.

Joe snorted. 'No, stupid. The tooth fairy only comes to children. Mummy doesn't need money.'

Rachel laughed and almost spat out the tissues.

'Mummy could *always* do with money,' she muttered. 'You two wait here. Don't get out. You'll be at school in five minutes.'

She pulled up outside a post box, then grabbed the letter, wiping the blood that had smeared a little on the envelope. She heard a click and a whoosh as it hit the pile of other letters in the box. It was a strange sound, one that was familiar but she couldn't quite place, until she turned around. Joe was aiming the gun of his action figure out the window and firing missiles at the pavement. As she made the few steps back to the car she trod on one of the small pellets. It dug right into the arch of her shoe-less foot. She tried not to yell, but a small squeak escaped her mouth.

'Mummy look out!' Claire said as Rachel hopped up and down, trying to avoid the pellet-covered pavement.

Claire's warning was too late and the boy on the skateboard didn't have time to veer out the way. They collided. Rachel fell to the ground, her wrist twisting under her as she smacked into the pavement. Now all she could do was groan.

'Are you alright?' the boy said, as he picked up his skateboard.

'I, I'm fine,' Rachel said. 'Owwww.'

She'd tried to use her hands to get up but a pain shot through her left wrist. She looked to the car. Her usually disobedient children had for once done what she asked and stayed where they were.

'What should I do?' the boy asked.

Rachel looked at him as she very inelegantly got to her feet. He looked no older than thirteen and his gelled hair had flopped in front of his worried face.

'It's fine. I'm fine. You should be at school shouldn't you?'

She recognised his uniform. It was the same as Luke's.

'If you're sure you're okay,' he said.

Rachel waved at him with her good arm and he backed away from her. She climbed into the car and placed her head on the steering wheel.

'Mummy?' Claire said quietly, after a few moments.

Rachel felt her daughter gently stroke her hair.

'It's fine. Mummy's okay,' Rachel said. But as she lifted her arm another searing pain went through her wrist. It was starting to swell.

'Joe,' Rachel said. 'Do you remember last summer when you sat in Grandad's car and he taught you the gear stick?'

'Naughty Grandad, you said,' Joe replied.

'Yes, well he was, but I'm going to need you to sit up front and help Mummy.'

'I want to. I want to. I want to!' Claire said, but Rachel ignored her.

Her swollen wrist lay useless in her lap and Joe's hand rested securely on the gear stick, waiting for her command. She drove most of the way in second gear, so he didn't have to do much, but she sweated profusely all the same. Five minutes later and they had made it to the school gates.

'Now have a good day,' she said to them as they clambered out the car. 'And remember, don't tell anyone about the school run.'

She watched as they ran through the gates with their large rucksacks bouncing on their backs. Once they were inside, she got out of the car. She'd have to call her boss again and tell her she wouldn't be in; her wrist was getting bigger by the minute. As she used the fingers on her good hand to scroll through her phone, she didn't see the flock of pigeons making their way overhead, nor notice the white shower raining down from them.

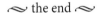 the end

ABOUT THE AUTHOR

Rebecca Perkin is a young adult fantasy and sci-fi author, who also loves writing short stories in various genres. Her writing evokes questions about the world around us and typically has strong female characters. Her self-published YA fantasy, White Plains, is available on Amazon. If you want to know more about her and what she has written visit www.rebeccaperkinauthor.com

You can also find her on Twitter @RebeccaPerkin where she tweets about writing and animals – her other passion!

How to Wake a Dragon

Brittany Muscarella

Once upon a time, in a kingdom far, far away, there lived–

No, my darling, *once upon a time* is just an old storytelling convention. This is a fairy tale, but it isn't *that* kind of fairy tale. You've never heard a story like this before, I promise you. Now. Once upon a time–

You're just as demanding as your mother when she was your age! I promise you: there are *no* knights in shining armor, *no* evil step-mothers or wicked witches, and there are *certainly* no helpless princesses trapped in towers waiting for charming princes to climb their hair and set them free! Now … may I *please* get on with the story, my dear?

Thank you.

Once upon a time, in a kingdom far, far away, there lived a princess who was, oh, just about your age. She looked a little bit like you, too. Her hair was just as long and just as black as yours.

This princess lived in a kingdom full of rolling hills and ancient fruit trees and clear blue streams. The biggest hill rose in the middle of the royal city, and the princess's castle sat right on top. Grey stones carved with mystical runes, an ancient draw-bridge that creaked on its way up and down, a deep green moat hiding all sorts of creatures that have never seen the light of day – you name it, this castle had it. This was the kind of kingdom that legends are made of. The sun always shone on the royal city, the most beautiful place in the world.

Well, the people who *lived* there thought it was the most beautiful place in the world, simply because they'd never seen the rest of it. In fact, there was one dark cloud over the castle and the city: the dragon.

Everyone in the kingdom knew about the dragon, though none of them had thought or spoken about it for a very long time. The dragon was the oldest creature in the world. It crawled up from the middle of the earth back in the beginning of time, when giants pushed their way out of their dark dirt homes into the sunlight. As the oldest creature, the dragon was also the most tired creature; it had slept for thousands and thousands of years with the end of its tail in its mouth, curled in a circle around the princess's kingdom.

Now, this might sound very magical and romantic to you or me, and I'm sure the scene would make a wonderful painting, but the dragon posed a problem. You see, the slumbering dragon created a giant, scaly, fire-breathing and flesh-eating barrier to the outside world. No one could come or go from the princess's city without waking the dragon.

I know what you're thinking. Couldn't a hero come along and defeat it so that the people could go out into the world? Well, it wasn't so simple, because this dragon could never be defeated, and you couldn't walk up to it without waking it, so there was no chance of sneaking past. Dragons are notoriously light sleepers.

Many ancient and renowned heroes from the princess's own city ventured forth to slay the dragon, but none ever returned. The dragon woke up, and the dragon went back to sleep.

Generations ago–

Yes, dear, long before even your old grandma was born–

A long, long time ago, this made the people of the kingdom very sad. They wanted to explore the world beyond the borders of their city. But as time passed and the dragon slept on, people forgot that they wanted to leave, so they stayed, and eventually they forgot that there *was* the rest of the world to explore.

Until the princess had her thirteenth birthday.

The princess's birthday was a party like no other in history. The king called in every acrobat, artist, bard, baker, blacksmith, cook, clothier, dancer, jester, juggler, jouster, minstrel, merchant, and merrymaker you can imagine. Tables piled high with rich food and drink lined the castle's great hall. Carts and wagons and rugs spread out in the cobbled courtyard held the artisans' finest creations, which the people purchased as gifts for the girl who would become their queen someday. There was dancing, and singing, and riddling, and storytelling; and it all lasted seven days and seven nights, until the princess's birthday came. Everyone was happy and no one thought about the world beyond the castle.

Then, on her birthday, the princess stood on her throne and thanked everyone very much for their thoughtful gifts and beautiful dances and wishes for good health. But the only gift she really wanted was missing from the piles of treasure they'd heaped at her feet. The people consulted each other. What had they forgotten?

Well, hadn't any of them ever wondered what lay beyond the walls of their kingdom … beyond the dragon? Some of the younger folk turned to their parents in confusion, and many of the parents wracked their brains to understand the princess's question. Eventually, they turned to the grandmothers, who narrowed their eyes and nodded their heads and tapped their chins as they remembered: yes, perhaps someone *had* mentioned something about a dragon once before, many, many years ago. A sleeping dragon keeping the kingdom captive.

That's the exact dragon the princess was speaking of! And she wanted to know what treasures lay far beyond its slumbering hide. Perhaps there was an ocean out there; the princess had always wanted to see an ocean.

An old man stood up and begged the princess to stay. The legends all said that this dragon couldn't be defeated. No matter the strength of the hero who went to wake it, he never returned, and the dragon always slept on.

The princess could at least approach the dragon to see what it was like, without waking it.

Dragons are notoriously light sleepers; it would wake up in an instant, the old man warned.

Oh, just let her go anyway, one grandmother said.

A general murmur arose from the people. Some doubted the dragon existed. Some feared what the old man said. Most feared what would happen once the edges of their kingdom touched the edges of the world.

But the princess wasn't afraid, and since no one would give her the gift of the world, she meant to go defeat the dragon herself. She left the next day.

The princess rode for days and nights through the land beyond the castle and city, until finally she reached the kingdom's end. A huge wall rose in front of her; its top disappeared into the clouds. The wall felt cool and rough to her touch. But it also felt alive.

The wall breathed: in and out, in and out, in time with the rise and fall of the princess's own chest.

She kept her hand on the wall as she walked along its length. For days and nights she walked, until the hide brought her to the face of the slumbering dragon. The dragon chomped down on its own long tail. Smoke curled from its nostrils. The creature purred like a cat having a pleasant dream. It seemed so happy and comfortable in its rest that perhaps she shouldn't wake it after all; just go back to her castle, let the dragon sleep on. She could visit an ocean another time.

All of a sudden, she was looking at another princess – just about the same age, with the same long black hair. This princess could have been her twin. Then the reflection was gone, and when it reappeared, the princess realized she was staring into a giant green eye. And it was staring back.

Before she could blink, the dragon spit out its tail and reared up on to its hind legs, as tall as it could get.

The princess stood taller, too.

The dragon snorted out two gusts of soot and smoke, covering her in black dust.

The princess let the ash settle in her hair.

The dragon bellowed into the sky, shaking the clouds until huge, fat drops of water splattered the princess's dirty face.

The princess welcomed the cleansing rain.

The dragon stomped its feet and swung its tail, rending the earth in two before it.

The princess stood with one foot on either side of the abyss.

The dragon roared, *who dares disturb my slumber?*

I've come to defeat you, the princess said.

I can't be defeated.

No one has tried hard enough.

The dragon chuckled: *You'll see what I mean.*

The dragon's last laugh left its mouth in a puff of smoke. The princess raised her sword, and the creature belched flame at the girl. The world burst into red and orange and white; the princess closed her eyes against the blast but never dropped her sword.

But when the fire, smoke, and dust settled, the princess was no longer there. The blast of fire from the creature's throat burned up everything in its wake just as crisp as you like. Only two footprints remained in the scorched earth. With a satisfied burp, the dragon closed her eyes.

When the princess opened her eyes, the world looked much smaller than she remembered, as if her head was in the clouds. She blinked. Her head *was* in the clouds: when she looked down, all she could see above the expanse of burnt ground was a stretch of shining, brilliant gold scales.

Dragon's scales.

She tested her dragon's wings. They weighed so much; the effort to move them exhausted her. She looked at her tail, curled far around the kingdom till its tip rested at her claws. Such a long way to travel. Following the path of her tail made her eyes heavy. She should go back to sleep. Maybe after she'd rested a bit she would fly.

Then, there, the sun glinting off the towers of her castle caught the dragon-princess's eye. She thought about the people who'd forgotten about the dragon, who'd forgotten about *her*. Her eyes opened wide and her nostrils flared. She flapped her wings again.

This time, she took off into the air, huge wings beating against the sky with a *whump*. The wind of her passage set worlds in motion. As she flew over her city, the people cried and the people screamed. They saw the dragon and they knew what it meant. The legends were true. The dragon could never be defeated. The poor princess, and only thirteen! They mourned her, taken from them by the creature's flame.

Yet in all the sorrow, the grandmother smiled. Perhaps the dragon could never be defeated, but this time the dragon was awake.

Higher and higher the dragon-princess flew until her kingdom was as small as a grain of sand below. She had never seen a grain of sand before, and wondered if, for all those years, her body had hidden an ocean out there. She swung her dragon's head back and forth, searching.

A shimmer of blue in the distance caught her green eye. It was a small glimmer; by the looks of it very far away. It would take a long time and a lot of flying to get there. And she'd been asleep for so long she couldn't tell if the vision was real or not. Maybe she'd get there and there would be nothing at all: no shimmer of blue, no ocean, no waves of endless sand–

Yes, dear, of course there is a happy ending. Because even though she might never see the sun sparkling on the waves of the sea, or feel the salt in the air cling to her wings like diamonds–

She thought she'd try anyway.

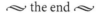 the end

ABOUT THE AUTHOR

Brittany Muscarella is a writer from Buffalo, NY. She lives with her husband in London, where she writes stories and takes long walks. You can follow Brittany on Twitter: @the_write_britt

How to Wake a Dragon was shortlisted and highly commended by the judges.

The Key

Carole Sleight

Nancy gripped the latch tightly, her knuckles white, and briefly let her forehead rest on the faded green paint. She was standing on the threshold of Sam's domain, preparing to go inside. She knew what to expect, after all, she'd been in on countless occasions and yet this time was different. Of all his worldly goods and effects, the shed was the final one to be sorted through; the last vestiges of Sam's life to be packed away, ready for removal. Every inch of the place was crammed with treasured tools and horticultural paraphernalia, garnered from years of tending the vegetables and flowers he loved. Dreading what was going to be one of her most difficult tasks, she had put it off until today.

Raising her head and squaring her shoulders, she opened the door and stepped into the dry, still interior. She inhaled deeply; the rich, peaty, potting compost aroma vividly transporting her back to walking in the woods with Sam and their dog. Rain pattered around them, his strong hand held hers, and the smell of damp earth was fresh and wholesome in her nostrils.

Sighing, she looked about. A few plant pots were clustered under the window and it took a moment before she recognised the withered brown stalks as Sam's cuttings, over-wintering out of the frost until he could plant them out. Irrationally, she felt guilty for abandoning them, even though she hadn't known they needed her care.

An old biscuit tin sat next to the pots and she ran a finger over the ridges and furrows of the embossed pattern on the lid. She had bought the assortment one Christmas, possibly fifteen years ago, when Sam's brother and his wife flew over to see them. She prised it open and found neat rows of seed packets lined up to support one another, some of which hadn't even been touched. She picked out a few and flicked through them; unexpected hot tears spilling over her eyelids at the sight of the used ones, prudently turned down in an effort to seal the tops again. They were covered with smudged, muddy fingerprints, those unique etchings of humanity that looked as fresh as if Sam had made them yesterday. A stabbing pain shot through her heart, so sharp it made her gasp as she encountered pictures of cornflowers, cosmos and sweet peas, all her favourite flowers. Sam grew them every year especially for her to cut and display in sparkling crystal vases on their windowsills. Slowly, she put them back and replaced the lid, taking care to return the tin to its former position. Sam liked to know where he could find things; everything had its place.

She extracted a tissue from one of the little packs she always carried with her nowadays and dabbed her eyes, wondering where she should start. There were seed trays, stacks of clean plant pots, bags of special compost; so many jars full of odd nails, screws, labels, pens, all sorts of things. There was even a small bag filled with neatly rolled oddments of string, stored until they came in useful for something. In fact, there was a whole collection of objects that she would probably never need.

Then her eye fell on his ancient padded waistcoat, hanging from a hook. Sam always wore it when he was working outdoors.

She tried to remember when she gave it to him; was it a birthday, or even the same Christmas that she bought the biscuits? Had it faded in the sun, or were the threads always this subtle blend of autumnal russet and orange tones?

Ashamed of the deficiency, she found she couldn't remember and to her, that felt like a betrayal of Sam. She wanted to hold every piece of their marriage in her heart forever, until the organ gave way and stopped beating under the sheer weight of recollection. Why did so many memories disappear beyond the reach of consciousness, sinking into the muddy silt at the bottom of the mind? How was it that these moments of her time with Sam were lost to her?

She stroked the faded tweed of the garment, reassuring herself. It didn't matter if she thought it used to be brighter, because from the moment it caught her eye in the shop window, she knew he would love it, and he did. He faithfully stuck with it, wearing it even when styles changed and he could have had something new. Images of him, happily working in the garden and wearing the waistcoat come flooding back to her, making her smile. It was true that many memories were buried, but she still had the best ones, shining radiantly in her mind with the clear, clean light of a fresh summer day at the seaside. But what was she going to do with the saggy old thing now? It was too old even for charity, no-one would possibly want to buy it. The wrench at her stomach when she supposed she would have to throw it away was like a physical blow and she thought, not yet. Every fibre contained a connection to Sam and she wanted to keep them for as long as possible.

Picking up the waistcoat, she clasped it to her chest, hugging it tight and felt an unexpected, rigid shape in one of the pockets. She slipped her hand into the folds of fabric and pulled out a heavy key, a worn leather loop attached to it and she caught her breath.

The key to Sam's allotment. Her fist closed on the metal in a fierce embrace as she stared across the lawn to the empty house. She hadn't realised that Sam might still have things stored down there and she was going to have to face going back, just to make sure.

It took more than a week for Nancy to gather her courage and set out for the allotment. She chose a mid-week morning when the working folk would be occupied, and hoped the light crisping of frost on the leaves might keep everyone else away, so she could visit without being seen. She pulled on her favourite red woollen beret to cover her short greying hair and walked to the end of the next street. From here, she could see the allotment site beyond a small park on the other side of the road. It was close to their home and she had often taken sandwiches or mugs of fresh tea over to share with Sam. Then they would talk happily about the crops, their progress and jobs yet to be done.

Crossing the deserted tarmac and muddy patch of green, she reached the metal-linked fence enclosing the plots. She slid through the gate and locked up again, pausing to glance around. There was no-one in sight and she walked briskly through, hands thrust deep in her pockets, her fingers restlessly spinning the key over and over as she went. She noticed with approval the signs of preparation for a new season, though it was only early March. Some had adopted an idea of Sam's; covering the ground with black polythene to warm the soil in anticipation of sowing seeds.

Nancy reached the site that used to be Sam's and stopped short, frowning. Newly turned clods of bare earth. Someone had been working here.

'I forked it over for you last week,' said a voice at her elbow.

Turning, she found herself facing Bob, his hooded, china-blue eyes watching anxiously for her reaction. Retired now, he had time to indulge his enthusiasm for gardening and life in general, and had been generous with offers of help when Sam became ill. Nancy was grateful for that kindness.

'Bob, I didn't see you or I would have come over.' She clasped his rough, square hand in her slim one and squeezed. 'How are you?'

'I'm fine, as always. I was in the shed, cleaning my fork.' He brandished the shiny implement for Nancy's inspection. 'I've been hoping to see you, Nancy, and when I spotted that hat, I knew it was you. How are you getting along? Everyone's been asking.'

His enquiries brought a lump to her throat, which she quickly swallowed.

'Oh, you know, not so bad,' she replied, with a slight shrug of her shoulders. She thrust her hands back into the pockets of her waxed jacket and considered the condition of her battered wellington boots. She changed the subject. 'Why did you dig the plot?'

'I couldn't bear to see it lying neglected. It looked out of place when the rest of us have made a start on ours.' Nancy swallowed another lump. Bob didn't need to remind her that Sam wasn't here to work his plot. 'I thought, if I turn the soil, when you take over it won't be such a big job.'

A flush of colour spread across her cheeks and she managed a little laugh as she shook her head. 'That's very nice, Bob, but I haven't thought about taking over, it wouldn't feel right. I'm planning to write to the Council and tell them the allotment can be given to someone else.'

She gazed at the uneven clumps, some dusted with a hint of frost, and was aware that Bob dropped his head and looked at his grimy hands, resting on the handle of the fork. He let the prongs settle into the ground, then he, too, gazed at the barren brown allotment in front of them.

Eventually he said in his soft voice, 'Sam wouldn't want the plot to go to someone he didn't know. What if they start using weed-killers? He'd hate that, after all the care he put into nurturing the soil. He would want you to look after it, Nan. He often told me how much he enjoyed it when you were here, tending the plants together.'

She nodded, unable to look Bob in the eye, not wanting him to see that she was close to tears. She rustled in her pocket for the pack of tissues, just in case, and to gain a moment to steady herself.

'Oh Bob, it's better to let it go to someone who can give it the attention it needs. You'll soon put them right about it being organic and chemical free. I simply can't imagine how I could ever keep it going, not on my own.'

'That's just the thing, Nancy. You don't have to do it alone. We've all said, each and every one of the holders, that if you take the plot on, we'll help you as much as possible. It's the least we can do, for Sam's sake, as well as yours. We're united in this. We want you to make a go of it. What do you say, Nan? What have you got to lose? Please think about it. We'd all love it if you said yes.'

Nancy couldn't speak, her voice choked by the emotions whirling around her mind. She was picturing the rectangle of soil as it used to be; covered with a tapestry woven of vegetables and flowers, a jam-packed, beautiful, bountiful place. She never dreamed that she would keep the allotment. In fact, she hadn't given the place a second thought. But as she considered it now, the bare ground seemed like a silent loom, inviting her to begin to weave, planting and creating her own pattern. A warmth spread through her veins, like the dawn creeping in, banishing the cold and illuminating the possibility of a new life. Maybe she thought, just maybe, she could do it. An image of Sam came to mind and a little smile touched her lips as she wondered whether that old waistcoat would fit her.

~ the end ~

ABOUT THE AUTHOR

Carole Sleight was born in South Yorkshire but now lives in Scotland with her partner. She is a psychological therapist. Carole writes poetry, short stories and longer works of fiction for both adults and children.

F for Finality

Dean Moses

I stand, surrounded by family and friends – pigtails dyed pink, dress wrinkled, and through dark, impenetrable shades I watch her descend into the earth – a trail of the crowd's melancholy following her like a sympathetic pat on the back.

My grandmother died last week. *Saving Grace Hospital* had become her tomb before she truly needed one. Day after day I sat, confined by white walls, across from the bed in which she lay, dust visibly dancing ahead of the open window, roses rotting on a nightstand, tubes jutting from her body like a broken puppet. She was a sight to behold before the end, a sight too sore for my eyes to shed. I've attempted to blink away that image, yet it has glued itself to the underside of my eyelids, a thick, gooey film. Her lingering death isn't even the worst part of it all, it's the possibility that she might have made it through the whole ordeal – seen more summer days and winter nights – but she didn't want to. She yearned to cast off her mortal coil and submit herself to heaven, at least her idea of it: the classic Sunday school version, a paradise too good to be true. It's not like she was a bad person, it's just that this notion of a perfect place in the sky should be reserved exclusively for the man in the street yelling: 'Jesus is coming' and 'The end is nigh!' Something about the idea of heaven has always made me nauseous, an imperfect world culminating in a perfect one. Sounds like bad fiction.

Since her death I have been considering the f-word far too frequently in such a small timeframe, the word my mother used at Grandma's funeral mere minutes ago: 'Finality. The finality of all things.' She's right. All things do have a beginning and an end. One year ago, I was hired at the local supermarket as a *shelf stocker extraordinaire*, and then, less than two months into my not-so-promising career, I threw three brown eggs at the manager when he tried to grope me in the stockroom, so I was fired. My job had finality, and so did Grandma.

As a woman in 2017, I wonder if the wage gap will ever have finality, if love and hatred have finality, if the universe has finality. These are the kinds of questions I should have pondered when I was a teenager draped in black eye shadow and inverted crosses. Perhaps I was too emotional back then; all wrapped up with pressure, with stress. The stress of teenage life, the pressure of school exams, not to mentation the promise of college looming just over womanhood's horizon. All I had back then was emotion, it was the adolescent's commodity with which to barter a better life from school professors. Now, with my school years not so distantly behind me, I am just emotional enough.

While I ride in the passenger seat, away from Grandma's lowered coffin and costly headstone, I hate my own thoughts for sounding like a philosophy student. Nevertheless, something about the strident, flat pitch of Grandma's heart monitor failing has left me in deep awe of the f-word, although I don't quite know why since I'm still young.

Grandma's death was no freak accident. A drunk driver didn't suddenly take her from us one wet and windy night. A mugger didn't get spooked and pull the trigger on a helpless old lady. We all knew it was coming; hell she welcomed it. My mom took the loss with a stiff upper lip, a stark disconnect allowing her to supervise the organized chaos. She stood up straight and calmly purchased the plot, ordered the flowers, and had the gravestone engraved. Now we drive, tombstones and crypts whizzing by – grey blemishes on the other side of the windshield. I think I want to be cremated.

'I'm hungry,' my mom calmly announces as she exits the graveyard. 'Want a burger? I could go for a *boat* load of fries right about now. And hot sauce.'

I do not look at her directly, but at her reflection in the glass, the shadow version of her, and the form I believe holds just as many conflicted feelings as I do. Maybe her sadness is trapped on the other side of that mirror image, begging to come out in a hail of shattering glass.

'Aren't you sad? Even a little?' My tone sounds rehearsed, as if I have been waiting to pick a fight. Even I pick up on this.

She sighs; a sigh reserved for mother and daughter talks. 'Of *course* I'm sad … I am also hungry. Can't I be both?'

She always liked to play the part of a strong, single mother. I can't tell if she is playing that game now, or if she is truly unfazed by the entire situation. When Dad left she acted like nothing had changed. She didn't miss a beat, helping me with my homework every night and cooking dinner, she even received a promotion for excelling at work – all during the court case. I didn't see her cry, not once. She did such a great job I hardly even knew Dad was gone. Nowadays, it's like he was never there at all.

'I guess you can. Though, one should come before the other.'

She opts to ignore this, fixing her eyes on the freeway, scanning every turn and side road in hopes of spying the elusive fast food. She seems more irritated than dejected, and that exacerbated resentment looks to be directed at me instead of the virus that stole her mother. I suspect this is due to my mopey demeanor. Does she feel bitter because I care more?

'There! I thought I would never find one.'

I follow her pointed finger with my eyes. Her favorite burger joint lies just over flaked nail polish. Her hand clenches into a fist, flourishing success in the small space between us.

I take a table beside the window – a scenic view of parked middle-income cars and splintering concrete – falling into the bolted-down seat. Being lunchtime, the place bustles with incoherent chatter. The hot smell of sizzling meat meets my skin, my pores becoming more and more sodden by the second. Mom orders our food with a smile; she is having a perfect day from the cashier's point of view. With my worn boots propped on an adjacent chair, I observe her bounce toward me, balancing two milkshakes on a tray – an android powered by the relentless mechanics of life – blissful and carefree despite the finality we have just endured. She plops a burger down in front of me. It oozes fat. A deceased creature lies stuffed somewhere between those buns, another prime example of the f-word.

'What have you got planned for the rest of the day,' Mom asks, before biting into her own burger.

It hits me, hard, like I am back in that hospital again – in that tomb – only this time it is bereavement encased in a mausoleum instead of Grandma. Mom's conviviality could be seen as admirable, but I see it as lack of compassion. I push the plate away.

'Why are we doing this? Pretending like everything is okay, I mean. Grandma is dead, that's not okay.'

She drops her half-eaten burger. It hits the paper plate with a resounding splat, flinging meat wads and spots of ketchup across the table. 'What do you want from me? She's gone to a better place. Do you think she would want us languishing in sorrow? She's at peace now. I just wish you and I could be, too.'

I bring white-knuckle fists down onto the table, slinging the morsels of food back her way. 'I think she would want us to care. She was your mother for God's sake!'

Mom says ... nothing. She stares wide-eyed, mouth ajar – shaken by my outburst. She thrusts herself up from the seat, backing away.

'Mom ...'

She falls to her knees in an explosion of screams and tears, her sombre makeup dissolving into a flowing river – the mirror-Mom has broken through the glass. The restaurant's humming prattle lowers to verbose gasps, its patrons stare. I rush to console her but she swats at me with flailing hands and press-on nails.

'I tried to be strong for you! ' Our eyes meet, I see my childhood waltz in her pupils. She wails, 'I want my *mommy*!'

I feel my heart break. This is the finality of my mom's motherly façade, the suit she had put on every day just to prevent me from feeling the finality of that awful f-word. With tears in my own eyes I meet her on the ground and wrap her within my arms.

∽ the end ∽

ABOUT THE AUTHOR

Dean Moses is a writer and photographer. He authored A Stalled Ox from 1888. His work has been featured in The Cost of Paper Volume IV and V from 1888, BONED Every Which Way 2016 and 2017: A Collection of Skeletal Literature from Spaceboy Books, and Grindstone Literary Services 2017 Anthology.

Poets & Writers:
https://www.pw.org/content/dean_moses
Facebook: https://www.facebook.com/deanlmoses/
Instagram: @dean.l.moses

Safe Passage

Laura Stump

The day was a pale lavender glimmer on the western horizon when the ship hove into view. Its single sail said 'Greece', but the unmistakable sounds from below decks said 'slavers'. Screams and moans, the cracks of whips, pleas for mercy. Agony reverberated through the hull and into the water, spreading for miles through the sea.

The sound called her up from the depths. The tips of her diaphanous fins undulated in the current as she stroked her way toward the ship's shadow. The sounds called others, too, as only misery and impending death did. She could see bulky bodies knifing toward her: the nautical harbingers of death, sharks. Smaller predators followed behind, trailed distantly by enterprising scavengers. Other creatures dove for cover, fearful of being caught in the hunt. The cavalcade of death stretched for nearly a mile.

Aeode hummed, filling the water with a discordant strain that the predators recognized as warning. They fell away, leaving her to stalk the ship on her own. This was her prey, and they would interfere at their peril. A siren was on the prowl.

The oceans had been her home since time immemorial, or so

it felt. She had seen generations of humans come and go, ferrying across the seas in an ever-evolving series of ships. Untold thousands had crossed her territory and many had died in it. What had endured through it all had been their cruelty toward one another.

To Aeode's mind, the on-shore cruelty of humans was abhorrent enough. Yet, compounding that, they seemed determined to spread their misery far and wide. And she would not allow her seas to be tainted.

The very thought filled her with fury. No creature deserved to live the horror those above her now did, any more than those responsible for inflicting such horror deserved to pass unscathed through her waters. No, there was a much more fitting fate for this ship, and no creature of the waves was more perfectly suited to change its direction than she.

Her course of action determined, Aeode put on a burst of speed that brought her level with the ship's bow. A sense of purpose and effort from those working diligently to keep the ship on track cut through the miasma of pain and suffering. Her music would reach them, and its magic would insinuate itself into their hearts until she held control over them all. They would be hers to command.

She raised her head to the sky, breaking through the swells and the spray. With a deep breath, the siren unleashed her song. She channeled all her rage at human cruelty into the music. The magic it called up wove itself through her melody to set tiny hooks in the sailors' minds, blinding them to everything but her.

Aeode's song pulled them on without remorse, even as the jagged rocks of her chosen stretch of coastline came into sharp relief against the fog. The ship continued on its course undeterred. When the razor edges ripped out its guts, the ship groaned like a wounded animal and floundered on to its side, one bank of oars waving in the air before crashing into the sea. Sailors were thrown from the decks and rigging, to be crushed on the rocks. Salt water poured into the hold, threatening to drown those who had survived the initial collision.

At the first impact, Aeode dove beneath the waves, arrowing her sleek body toward the breaches in the hull. She could hear a cacophony of terror, confusion, and pain. A limp body floated toward her, blood from rent flesh darkening the water. She steeled herself, knowing it would be but one of many she must ignore to focus on survivors.

Time and again she seized struggling figures, pulling them from the ocean. She breathed life into them when the water threatened to squeeze it from them. She deposited them with care on the sand of a nearby beach before diving in for more.

She lost count of how many still-breathing bodies she dragged to safety, even as she struggled to avoid the grasping hands of those finding the tables turned after so recently delighting in the misery of others. One lunged from a floating spar and wrapped his arms around her tail, clinging like a limpet. Unable to shake him, Aeode swam toward the seabed. The sailor held on desperately as the sounds of the surface faded. By the time he realized his mistake and turned to claw his way to fresh air, it was too late. Aeode used his tactic far more effectively, holding his legs as he flailed. When he finally went limp, she discarded him and returned to the ship.

As the sun crept over the horizon, an eerie silence fell over the area, broken only by the crashing of waves against rocks and wreckage. By Aeode's reckoning, all those responsible for the agony that had drawn her had drowned, either on their own or with her assistance. The wails and sobs of the enslaved had subsided too; despite her best efforts, most never escaped the flooding hold.

Aeode pulled herself on to a looming spire of basalt. Below her floated wooden planks, barrels, lengths of rope, limp bodies; the sad detritus of a shipwreck. No heads or hands struggled to break into the air. It was over.

The crunch of feet and hands on crumbling rock startled her, and she rose to balance on her lower body like a snake. A bedraggled man hauled himself up, tunic tattered and knuckles bloody, the stench of cruelty rolling from him like fog off the sea at night.

'Why?' His voice was raspy with seawater. 'Why would you do this?'

Aeode turned cold black eyes on him. 'Why would I divert you from inflicting misery? Or why would I make sure none of you were left to try again? The ocean may be dispassionate, but you humans make her appear benevolent by comparison. It is live or die beneath the waves, but living is free of deliberate cruelty.'

The man sneered up at her. 'What would you know of human life, sea witch? You spend your life luring innocent men to their deaths in your cold embrace.'

'Oh, yes, those who willingly helped you spread misery and death were quite innocent, weren't they?' Aeode's laughter could have frozen the spray from the waves. 'Feeling, smelling, and tasting emotion is as natural to me as scenting blood is to a shark. All those on board who were truly innocent, I fought to save. Their despair and fear were easy to distinguish from the bitter anger and cruelty of those who were not.' She loomed over him, claws springing forth on webbed hands.

He shoved himself upright. His body bore testimony to the battering he had taken against the rocks, covered as it was with scrapes, cuts, and blossoming bruises. 'You have no right to judge me or my men, you bitch!' His face contorted in a snarl of rage, and he flung himself at her.

The impact of his body knocked them both off the rock and

into the sea. Aeode's tail grated against the basalt, leaving streaks of scales and blood. She snarled at the pain as the water crashed over them.

Beneath the waves, she unleashed a screech of pain and anger, buoying it with her magic. The percussive force of it slammed into the man, breaking his grip and forcing the air from his lungs. As she took stock of her injuries, he floated for a few seconds, dazed, before he shook his head and stroked upward.

Aeode followed. His head broke the surface in the space between two swells long enough to take a deep, ragged breath. Then she was on him again, digging the claws of her left hand into his calf, flipping herself and dragging him into the deep. Searing pain scored her fin. She looked over her shoulder in time to see him thrust a small but viciously sharp knife into the strong muscles of her tail. Ichor from her wounds and blood from his swirled in the churning water around them.

The siren snapped her tail away from him, jerking the knife still lodged in her body from his grasp. The move propelled them both sideways, her hooks in his leg drawing his lower body where she pleased. The man's arms wind-milled as he tried to fold his upper body against the current toward her.

His strong hands closed on hers, seeking purchase between her fingers and his leg. Strengthened by years at sea, he gained purchase enough to pry free one claw. But Aeode could feel his growing urgency: He, unlike the siren, needed fresh air, unadulterated by water. Her mouth split into a grin lined with needlelike teeth.

Aeode retracted the claws on her left hand as he struggled. The move freed his leg, but, before he could swim away, she tangled her right hand through his curly black hair. He realized his peril too late and could not fight the resistance of the water in time to avoid her grasp. One powerful flick of her tail – she

screamed at the pain from the knife still embedded in her flesh –
and she spiraled through the water, snapping his neck.

As daylight touched the island's shores, the surviving former
slaves clung to one another. The incoming tide brought them
scraps of wood and a few precious barrels of supplies. One by
one, they regained some sense of equilibrium and began to move,
thanking the gods for this second chance at life. Two older
women rallied the others, sending some in search of water and
setting others to work building shelter.

Neither woman was all that surprised when the captain's
body washed in with the tide; they had already set one of the
surviving men to disposing of dead bodies. They were, however,
startled by the figure who followed him, exhaustion and pain
stamped on its face. The creature dragged itself from the surf
on to the sand, leaving a trail of ichor and scales behind it. It
looked at them and smiled before reaching to pull a knife from
its tail, which it dropped into the surf before turning to head
back into the sea.

'Wait!' one of the women called, breaking into a trot toward
the shoreline. 'Please, wait!'

The creature paused. As the woman drew closer, it lowered
its body, careful of the rends in its tail but seeming desirous not
to frighten her.

The woman slowed. 'You saved us.'

A weary smile rounded the creature's cheeks. 'I am sorry I
could not save you all and sorrier still that you were here in need
of saving at all.' It paused, then drew a deep breath and continued,
'No one will disturb you here. Few humans know this island exists
at all, and most of those know that it lies under my protection. It

is not your home, but it is hospitable. And, if you wish, I can send word to your homeland so they can send a ship to retrieve you.'

'No!' The woman saw surprise in the creature's eyes. She wondered at her own vehemence but added, 'We shall make our lives here.'

The creature tilted its head. 'Why would you wish to remain here rather than return home?'

The second woman approached and answered for the first. 'Because they are the ones who sold us.'

The women stared in fear as grey lids fell over the creature's coal-black eyes. They had never seen such sudden anger. But as they drew back, they saw the creature struggle to control its emotions. It seemed to take an effort of will but eventually the creature smiled again. 'Then you can make your home here. This island will belong to you '

It turned to the surf. 'I shall visit you here from time to time. You will not be alone.' The two women watched as waves crashed against the creature's body as it waded out and, once deep enough, slid beneath the water and disappeared.

On the now-empty beach, the two women stood in silence. After a long moment, they turned their backs as one on the body of their former captor and walked inland to start their new lives.

$\sim$ the end $\sim$

ABOUT THE AUTHOR

A common worker droid by day, Laura Stump spends her evenings with comics, science fiction, and fantasy. Her first comic, with art by Jessica Trevino, appeared in the February 2018 anthology *Strange Romance*. She also writes for Women Write About Comics http://womenwriteaboutcomics.com. Follow Laura on Twitter at @LauraMStump or on her website at https://lauramstump.wixsite.com/portfolio

Princess Genevieve's Infinite Choices
A Choose-Your-Own-Adventure Fairy Tale

Jenna Samuels

1. The village of Talkeetna is neither wealthy nor powerful, but its residents are renowned for their friendliness and cheer. Farmers bring their neighbours fresh vegetables, pub-goers get drunk but never boisterous, and King Clarence is beloved by all. His daughter, Princess Genevieve, is even more celebrated for her beauty, kindness, and decision-making skills; countless men and women dream of her hand in marriage, even those on the other side of nearby Mount Infernon.

However, the past week, citizens of Talkeetna have observed a dark cloud gathering over the mountain, and slowly approaching their village. As the cloud approached, stranger and stranger events caused the citizens to worry: the bakery burned down, dogs barked through the night, and Mr and Mrs Crowley got into a big fight in the town square, and they never fight. The day it reached Talkeetna, the citizens looked up in fear. The town had never been so dark! Soon, crops started dying, cows stopped producing milk, and the villagers seemed to lose their usual cheer. Princess Genevieve promised her distraught subjects that she would lift the curse and restore Talkeetna to its former jollity. She suspected the curse was cast by Smaragdus the emerald dragon, who lived atop Mount Infernon, so she prepared a pack big enough to hike to Mount Infernon to speak to, and possibly fight, Smaragdus. The citizens asked, 'Why isn't the King going to save us?' but she ignored them and continued to prepare her pack. The truth is, King Clarence was terribly afraid of dragons. The next morning, Genevieve had a big breakfast and set off to:

- ask help from Sir Christopher, the village's bravest knight. Go to 2.
- climb Mount Infernon to confront Smaragdus. Go to 3.
- seek counsel from the witch, Bernadette, despite her suspicious reputation. Go to 4.

2. Sir Christopher's house was decorated with shiny medals and the furry faces of game he'd killed. When Genevieve asked for his help, he replied with a deep bow, 'I would do anything to help you, my Princess. As you know, I've defeated two dragons already.' He stood up tall and smiled proudly. 'I only ask one thing in return: your hand in marriage.' Princess Genevieve considered his offer. She didn't know him very well, other than that he was very handsome and brave, so she:

- reluctantly agreed. Go to 5.
- rejected Sir Christopher, and:
  - decided to save Talkeetna herself. Go to 3.
  - sought counsel from the witch, Bernadette. Go to 4.

3. Clutching her sword and enough food for the journey, Genevieve trekked for days, barely escaping an avalanche and a gang of trolls. On the third day, she saw the green dragon sitting atop the mountain. Sword drawn, she approached Smaragdus from behind, but hesitated when she heard the emerald dragon's weeping. Genevieve could not believe such a

large, powerful dragon could look so sad and weak; everyone said dragons were heartless! She:

- asked Smaragdus, 'Are you alright?' Go to 8.
- took advantage of the distraction and used this opportunity to charge. Go to 9.

4. Bernadette's home was cluttered with animal skins and vials of potions, which made Genevieve wary. Without introduction, the witch said, 'You plan to fight a dragon,' and drew an old, simple sword, promising, 'This weapon will give you the strength you need to kill Smaragdus and any other dragon you may come across.' Genevieve reached for the sword, but Bernadette pulled it back and warned, 'Even with this sword, the dragon's emerald scales are impenetrable. The sword demands a sacrifice from its user, and only the blood of a true warrior will satisfy it.' 'You mean I must cut myself before I fight Smaragdus?' The witch squinted her eyes and nodded. Genevieve wasn't sure she believed Bernadette, she had heard the witch was losing her mind:

- but she took the sword and thanked her anyway. Go to 14.
- so she politely declined the witch's sword:
  - and decided to ask Sir Christopher for help instead (if he was still alive). Go to 2.
  - and took off for Mount Infernon with her own sword. Go to 3.

5. They embraced, and kissed awkwardly. Genevieve admired Christopher's courage and confidence, but she feared that she would lose her new fiancé, and the kingdom's best soldier, if he tried to fight Smaragdus on his own. 'I will go with you,' she said, but Christopher insisted the princess must remain in her castle where she would be safe, so:

- she rolled her eyes and left, breaking their engagement. Go to 3.
- she waited for Christopher to leave and then sneakily followed him to Mount Infernon. Go to 6.
- she gave Christopher her favourite locket for good luck. Go to 7.

6. After a long, treacherous journey, Christopher reached Mount Infernon's peak, and Genevieve followed, hungry and tired, but still unseen by her fiancé. They were both shocked to find Smaragdus, covered in beautiful emerald scales, weeping atop her hoard of treasure. Sir Christopher laughed and jeered. 'Crying? I thought dragons were supposed to be tough.' Smaragdus stopped crying, looked at him, and immediately engulfed him in her angry flame. Genevieve, though shocked and terrified, still managed to:

- draw her sword. Go to 9.
- ask Smaragdus what was upsetting her. Go to 8.

7. Genevieve waited and waited for news of Sir Christopher, as the town continued to suffer under Smaragdus's curse. One day, a crow arrived at her window with her locket, burned and scratched, as well as one shining emerald scale. Sir Christopher had been killed. Genevieve:

- clutching the locket, threw herself from the window of her tower. Go to 15.
- knew she must save Talkeetna herself. Go to 3.

8. Smaragdus woefully admitted, 'I'm sorry Princess Genevieve. You were right, the curse *is* my doing! Every village in this region is appointed a dragon protector, and I've been Talkeetna's guardian for centuries, shielding your town from

all sorts of evils and curses sent by other dragons. But your town's fate – weather, crops, business, even the villagers' cheer – depends on my mood. For centuries, I've forced myself to be lighthearted and happy, for Talkeetna's sake, but lately I've become so sad.' She sobbed. 'My two best friends were killed by a knight last year, and I've been lonely without their visits.' Genevieve advanced, and hugged Smaragdus's enormous right cheek, shining and slick with tears. She noticed a spot behind the dragon's ear that was not covered in scales; it looked soft and vulnerable, almost like a human's skin. She:

- saw her opportunity to strike. Go to 10.
- gently kissed Smaragdus on the exposed skin. Go to 11.

9. She sneaked up on the dragon and tried to stab her in the back of the head, but her sword ricocheted off the shiny scales, creating a spark. Smaragdus turned to her, violently angry now, and Genevieve barely ducked in time to avoid her sharp fangs. She thrust at the dragon again and again, dodging Smaragdus's blows, but her sword still could not penetrate the emerald scales. Exhausted and bloody, Genevieve was about to give up when she glimpsed Smaragdus's hoard of treasure. She grabbed a handful of gold, certainly enough to buy new crops and cows for Talkeetna, and:

- turned to escape down the mountain. Go to 12.
- threw it off the cliff. Go to 13.

10. Genevieve swiftly pierced her sword into the dragon's neck, and Smaragdus, deeply wounded, breathed angry fire. Genevieve retrieved her sword and ducked behind a boulder just in time. Go to 9.

11. The moment her lips touched the emerald dragon, Smaragdus was surrounded by swirling green smoke, and instantly transformed into a stunning woman, with eyes as green as her scales had been. Staring at her hands in disbelief, Smaragdus cried, 'It's been so long since I was turned into a dragon, I can barely remember being a woman. I feel so free! Genevieve, your compassion has transformed me. Thank you!' The two women embraced. Go to 18.

12. The trees became a blur as Genevieve raced down Mount Infernon. After she had run for about an hour, her lungs were burning and her legs were sore, but she felt confident that she'd escaped. With no dragon in sight, Genevieve slowed to rest, certain that Smaragdus was wounded and tired from their earlier battle. Suddenly, she heard the thrash of wings and felt a shooting pain through her abdomen, as bloody, emerald jaws pierced her middle. Go to 16.

13. Smaragdus shrieked and flew off the mountain to chase her fortune, for she was famously greedy. Taking a running start, Genevieve leapt on to the dragon's back, circling her arms around the thick, flailing, green neck. There it was, a small spot of skin, unprotected by scales, behind the dragon's left ear. Pulling back, she stabbed her sword into this weak spot, as deep as it would go. Go to 17.

14. Genevieve travelled up the mountain with the sword that might be magical, or might leave her practically defenceless. After three days of trekking, she reached Mount Infernon's peak and found Smaragdus, whose luminescent scales enticed and nearly blinded her. She ducked behind a large, leafy tree, and, ignoring her fear, drew her sword, slicing it into her own hand. The cut was deep, and the sword was quickly covered in Genevieve's blood. She was so nervous about fighting Smaragdus that she barely felt the wound. Soon, the sword started to glow red and Genevieve smiled. The witch had been telling the truth. Genevieve wrapped her hand and charged at the dragon. Upon seeing the magical red sword, Smaragdus began to tremble and beg for mercy. Genevieve:

- pitied the dragon and sheathed her magic sword. Go to 8.
- ignored the dragon's pleas and charged. Go to 9.

15. Flying through the air, Genevieve deftly grabbed the closest branch and climbed to the ground, without even tearing her dress. She shook her head, wishing Sir Christopher hadn't been so reckless, although it was nice to have her favourite locket back. Examining the unbreakable, shimmering emerald scale, Genevieve knew she was in for a tough fight. Go to 3.

16. Smaragdus, satisfied with her delicious meal, retrieved her stolen gold and returned to the top of Mount Infernon, where she happily lifted the curse. Almost immediately, the sky brightened, and all of Talkeetna's worries faded back into the past. Every year, even to this day, the citizens of Talkeetna celebrate the sacrifice their Princess Genevieve made for their town. Go to 19.

17. Smaragdus thrashed and screamed, but started to fall. Genevieve leapt from the dragon's back and reached out, taking hold of a stray branch. She pulled herself to safety and wiped the sweat off her face, panting. She slowly began the journey back to her village. When she returned, she saw at once that Talkeetna's curse had been lifted. The villagers threw a grand party to celebrate her victory. The dark cloud never returned to Talkeetna's skies again. Go to 19.

18. Genevieve and Smaragdus returned to Talkeetna, and married a few years later. The two ruled in glory well into their old age, and Smaragdus, whose mood still dictated the fate of the village, was so happy in her marriage to Genevieve, that there was nothing but joy and prosperity throughout the land. Go to 19.

19. Talkeetna never suffered again under the curse of a dragon.

∽ the end ∽

ABOUT THE AUTHOR

Jenna Samuels lives in Queens, New York, teaching English by day and selling fish by night. In between, she writes stories about adventurous, intersectional goofballs. She has an MA in Creative Writing from Edinburgh Napier University, and is engaged to marry Queen Genevieve's son in July 2019. Twitter: @JennaLSamuels

Acts of Courage

Alan Paine

Anita sat on the towel Joe had spread on the sand and wondered if she would have the nerve to do what she had planned. It was the bravest thing she had ever considered and she wasn't sure that she could go through with it. She closed her eyes and breathed in the sea air, trying to calm her churning stomach. Joe put his hand gently to the back of her neck. 'You don't have to do this if you don't want to,' he said.

'Yes I do. I said I would and I'm not going to back out now. I just need a few minutes.'

Would this really be the bravest thing she'd ever done? What about the courage it had taken to stand up to that useless husband of hers? In what now seemed like another lifetime, she had been happily married. Or so she'd thought. But she knew now it had been an empty shell. She hadn't been happy at all. Although she'd not experienced the depths of total despair either until that fateful day. Bravery had been the last thing on her mind. Her thoughts reached back to touch the shock and disbelief of her husband's abandonment at just the point she needed him most. Now she knew she'd never really needed him and she savoured the relief of being free from his controlling influence.

As everything in her previously stable life had collapsed around her in shards, she'd been ready to let him walk away and leave her with nothing. Then, from somewhere, she had found a spark of self-respect in the darkness. She'd screwed up her courage and faced him in court. She could still remember her trembling hands and the taste of sick in her mouth. It hadn't been to punish him, just to get a fair share of what they had built up during their time together. Her lawyer had seemed a little disappointed with the final deal but Anita had been elated. It hadn't been a victory over him, but a victory over herself. She'd found the nerve to do something to start climbing out of the pit.

Her next act of bravery had been to tell Joe why her husband had left her.

She and Joe had started off as car pool friends. Anita lived the furthest from the office so she always drove, while Joe and Fiona shared the cost of the petrol. After dropping off Fiona one evening, they got stuck in traffic. It took over an hour to reach Joe's house, yet the easy conversation had made the time fly by. She'd seen Joe's reluctance to get out of the car and felt thrilled when he'd said, 'Come in for a coffee.'

Coffee led to dinner, which became drinks on the settee, until she knew she'd drunk too much to drive home. It felt amazing when they kissed, but she was suddenly gripped by fear and reacted angrily the moment he tried to take things further, roughly pushing off his tentative move.

'It's OK, Anita.' She saw him try to hide his disappointment as he stood up, and felt desolate as he moved away.

Thoughts swirled in her head and she didn't feel the least bit sleepy, but the next thing she remembered was waking up on the settee with a blanket over her. She checked the time; it was three in the morning. I've just rejected the nicest man I've met in years and then passed out on him, she thought. She went upstairs to the bathroom and as she was coming out, Joe called to her from his bedroom. 'Anita, is that you?'

'No, it's Fiona come to check up on you. Who did you think it was?'

'Well you never know, do you?'

'Would you rather it was Fiona instead of me?'

'Of course not.'

She wondered if he meant it. 'I feel such an idiot for falling asleep on you like that and … and for the other stuff.'

'Don't worry, it's alright.'

'Thanks, Joe. Well, I'll get back downstairs and let you get some sleep.'

'No, I can't allow you to sleep on that settee. There's a bed made up in the spare room.' He paused. 'Unless you want to get in with me.'

'Uh …' Anita's heart leapt, but fear pulled her back. 'Thanks, I'd … The spare room'll be great.'

She didn't sleep at all for the rest of the night. Her mind kept returning to his offer and what it would have meant for her to accept it. Before dawn, she got up and crept out of the house. There was time to drive home, get changed and then turn up at Joe's at the normal time as if nothing had happened.

He climbed in without a word and they drove to Fiona's. 'Are you OK, Anita?' said Fiona. 'You look really tired.'

It was clear that Fiona had sensed something was wrong, but fortunately, she let it lie and the journey continued in unusual silence.

The three of them repeated the same silent journey that evening, saying goodbye to Fiona who left looking troubled.

As Anita pulled up at Joe's, she tried to will him to speak. Though he said nothing, he seemed reluctant to get out of the car. She knew it was up to her to make the first move.

'Joe … I'm sorry how I acted last night. It's been difficult the last few years. I got divorced and I've … well, I've had some other problems.' She took his hand and gently squeezed it. 'I really like you and think you like me too. But … there's something you have to know.' She took a deep breath but the words stalled at the back of her throat. She couldn't say it. 'Would it be OK if I came in and we talked inside?'

The next few hours fell into the same groove as the previous evening. They talked effortlessly over dinner, instinctively drawn together until they were back on the settee with drinks again. He smiled at her. 'What's this something that I have to know?'

She pulled in a breath and felt tears welling up in her eyes. It was now or never. If he froze the way her husband had she would be utterly crushed. Could he possibly still want her after he knew?

The next morning, which was fortunately a Saturday, she woke up beside him and had to think for a few moments to remember what had happened. Yes, she'd told him everything and he'd just hugged her and said it was no problem.

'You looked lost in thought there for a minute.' Joe smiled and sat down on the towel beside her, his gaze roaming the crowded beach down to the blue of the sea.

'I was thinking about the times in my life when I've been frightened of doing something and after I've done it everything has been fine. But this is the most terrifying ever.'

'You'll be alright, don't worry.'

'OK then, here goes,' and she quickly pulled off her T shirt, removed her bra and then immediately crossed her arms over her chest. The noise of the crowd rumbled on around them; there was no sudden hush, no shocked intake of breath.

After a moment, a beach ball landed at her feet; a small girl running after it, her father at her heels. Anita uncrossed her arms, picked up the ball and tossed it to the girl with a smile. The girl grabbed it and raced off. Her father threw Anita a word of apology and thanks as he turned back, his focus on his daughter. Neither of them had reacted to her with the shock that she had expected. She looked around. A few people were glancing in her direction but no one was looking disgusted or covering their children's eyes.

She sat there topless, a scar where her right breast had once been, and no one gave her a second look. She almost felt cheated and couldn't help laughing.

This was a clothing-optional beach in Spain. There were people fully dressed, people completely naked and everything in between. The holiday had been a snap decision. It had surprised everyone in the office except for Fiona, who couldn't have failed to notice the magical change that had come over them after their first weekend together, or their surreptitious kiss in the car park before going to their separate departments.

'I'd never have set foot on a beach like this before my operation,' said Anita, 'dressed or not. But it's just the same as every other time. Whenever I've been scared shitless about doing something, I've felt so much better once I've done it. I'm sitting here showing off my damaged body and now I'm wondering what the fuss was about.' She hugged him impulsively. 'I'll never forget how nice you were when I told you. I can't believe how frightened I was that I'd lose you. My ex treated me like something the cat dragged in from the moment I was diagnosed. Couldn't cope with the thought of cancer. I was too ill to see that that was *his*

97

problem. I felt like I wasn't a woman any more. I got so low I might have ended it all.'

'I hate thinking about you being so ill and depressed,' said Joe, 'but if it hadn't happened then we wouldn't be together and I hate the thought of that as well.'

'Don't feel bad,' she said, 'sometimes you have to wade through the crap of life to get to the good stuff. People talk about the battle with cancer but it's not just the physical battle. That side's mostly down to the doctors. It's the mental battle they can't always help you with. I've had the all clear, but in my mind it's still a work in progress. I used to try not to look at myself in the shower. It was a big step the first time I let you see me without my bra on and just look at me now.'

'I can't get enough of looking at you. You know that,' he said.

She laughed again. 'I want to start talking about it, maybe helping others. There shouldn't be this stigma about having cancer. I was sick and I got better. It's nothing to be ashamed of. Having a part of your body missing is nothing to be ashamed of either. I could have had reconstructive surgery but I turned it down'

'Do you ever regret that?'

'No, why? Do you think I should have something done?'

'Of course not. Not unless you want to.'

'Well I don't. I never liked the idea of implants or of having bits and pieces transferred from one part of my body to another. Back then I didn't even feel I was worth it. The nearest I came to regret was that night in your spare room. A part of me longed to be "normal" again so that I could get into bed with you. I didn't sleep a wink.'

'Neither did I. I was very tempted to go in and join you.'

'It's a good job you didn't. I'd probably have freaked out and never wanted to see you again.'

Joe kissed his hand, touched it against her scar and then her breast. Anita brought his fingers to her mouth and ran her lips and teeth across them, closing her eyes. Then she leant back with her hands behind her enjoying the warmth of the sun on her body. 'You know what,' she said, 'I get such a buzz from doing stuff that terrifies me I think I might try bungee jumping next.'

$\sim$ the end $\sim$

ABOUT THE AUTHOR

Away from his work as a chemical engineer in the edible oil industry, Alan Paine enjoys writing, painting and making music. He also acts and writes sketches with his local amateur theatre group. He lives in Dartford, Kent with his wife Jane and they have three children and three grandchildren.

Bioluminescence

Louisa Morillo

Disgust? Pity? Towards *me*? *Really*?

Ha. Land animals. So full of themselves. So full of air … Now, I'll hold up my fins and admit that this is all hearsay – I've never been up there, thankfully – but I've caught current of many a rumour about the surface. Its inhabitants have obvious peculiarities, an ability to breathe with no water for one thing, but above all they seem horribly *shallow*. They fixate upon aesthetic matters. As I say, this is all word-of-gill, but I've heard that their mating rituals are nothing short of bizarre. They partake in garish visual displays under the blinding sunlight. Feathers, manes, swaying buttocks, bulbous teats … Preening, strutting, quarrelling … I'm surprised they've any time left for actual procreation. The minute they hit maturity, thoughts of their bodies occupy their every waking moment. The atmospheric pressure may be considerably lower than it is down here, but the pressure on these land animals is, by all accounts, crushing.

This is why I shan't be shedding too many tears over its inhabitants' opinion of me. Apparently, I have been crowned 'world's ugliest creature'. The title does not preoccupy me. Don't be fooled by my translucence; we anglerfish are thick of skin, not easily affronted. I may lack allure but given that I possess an *actual lure,* I don't feel too deprived. What a waste of time it must be to have to pursue the food oneself. Acquiring a piece of animal corpse as a means of feeding oneself demands time, effort, planning. Meanwhile I need only dangle my lovely lure in front of my 'hideous' teeth and, with a little help from some bioluminescent bacteria, my dinner swims to me. This frees up my time considerably, enabling me to enjoy the peaceful darkness of the ocean floor, pondering matters much more profound than breeding and feeding. As an anglerfish, I'm a lucky lady indeed.

I wish I could say that the males of my species enjoy a similarly languid existence; alas, they do not. Some of those on the surface apparently refer to females as 'the weaker sex', as if childbearing and monthly bleeding and endless petitions for equality in the wake of millennia of subjugation are pastimes of the feeble. Down here, however, there exists not one drop of hegemonic masculinity. It is the females who are revered. Male anglerfish, bless them, are sadly lacking in luminous lures. The little chap swims up to me and, with one dainty love bite, he and I become one – quite literally. Squeamish, shallow inhabitants of the shallows, look away now; his body fuses into mine until all that remains of him is a pair of gonads adorning my side, which I can use to fertilise my eggs. This is apparently 'gruesome'. I'd argue that it's just a very authentic means of 'mating for life'.

I find myself bothered by the occasional 'deep-sea diver'. These creatures, not content with voicing their distaste for my visage from afar, encroach upon my space with their garish flashing cameras and rough plastic flippers, disturbing the dark tranquillity I so relish. I've heard ghastly stories about things called 'nature documentaries' which apparently require entire fleets of these masked neoprene horrors.

Given the intrusion, the insults, it would be justifiable for an anglerfish to harbour some ill will towards these ungracious beings. Truthfully, however, I feel only frustration and pity. I am frustrated because I think their time and resources would be far better spent combatting the shallowness of the shallows, a place where one's value and enjoyment of life are contingent upon one's aesthetic appeal above all else. I pity them because they are a sorry spectacle indeed, their head-torches nothing more than a pathetic prosthetic in a kingdom – no, *queendom* – of biolumi-nescent appendages. They can't bring their demands for facial symmetry and smooth skin and pointy footwear down here to *my* seabed. Quite frankly, if I may be blunt, with all the gonads I've accumulated so far, I have more balls than any of them.

 the end

ABOUT THE AUTHOR

Louisa Morillo has wanted to be a writer since she learned to read. She is now 20 and is studying Law at university. In her free time she enjoys entering short story and poetry competitions and is currently working on her first novel.

The Beholder

Lauren Everdell

She was a tasty piece, and it'd been a long day. Exhausting and fetid with Sergei in the passenger seat troffing cheese and onion crisps, smelling like hell's own armpit. I wanted a smile, that's all. Friday night, no work in the a.m, clocked-off and headed for the pub to meet the guys. Looked to be a solid night. Beers, friends, maybe a bird or two. I wanted a smile, that's all.

'What about that one, Mikey? Nice pair.'

'Nah.' I followed his greasy fingertip to a woman on the far pavement. 'Those're fake. Bony arse gives 'em away. Who'd want that on their lap? This one's got a nice set of legs on 'er, though. Wouldn't mind them wrapped round my waist.' I nodded in my choice's direction. Sergei made a humming, chewing sound of agreement.

'I prefer 'em small, though. She's tall as a bloke,' he said. 'Now this one. This one'll do.' He stuck his head out the window, aimed a swooping whistle at the woman. Thinking back on it, she was almost a girl still. A blast of car horns called my mind back to the road. The queue had rolled forward. I caught up. That's when I saw her.

A tasty piece, as I said. Though … I forget the details. Blonde hair, I know that. It's what snagged my eye, swinging with her strut like a gold rope, side to side across her back. Made me think of wrapping it around my hand like a boxer's bandage. I leaned out my window.

'Hey love, show us that pretty smile,' I said, Sergei laughing at my back. Crunching chips and laughing. 'Hey! I said smile for me, gorgeous.' She stopped. She turned.

'Oi oi,' Sergei jeered. I looked over my shoulder to grin at him and when I turned back she was framed in the eye of my window. What I remember is her lips. Red like the guts of a cherry pie. Red like the films of my eyelids, closed against the sun. Red like the bands in a milksnake's skin. She didn't use them to smile. She used them to shape the words she spoke.

'Please,' she said. 'Don't look at me.'

'What the–?' She'd already walked away.

'What'd she say?' Sergei's elbow landed in my ribs. I reached for the gearshift.

'Nothin.'

Most of the guys were waiting at the pub when we got there. We banged in a few rounds. Boys on good form, full of steam from a heavy week and keen to blow it off. Thought I caught a couple of them eyeing me though. When my turn came again I headed for the bar, leaning on the tacky varnish holding my wallet where the barman'd see it. I turned my eyes to soundless football on the TV. My mind filled with glistening white teeth sheathed by a pair of red lips.

'Please. Don't look at me.' I spun round, sure the breath of her voice caressed my ear. I scanned the people packed in at my elbows. Stocky, paint-marked guys like me. Stringy, Lycra'd cyclists. Rumpled, tie-loosened office guys and melted-makeup office girls. Chubby girls in strappy tops and sunburned guys in dorky sandals. Tourists. Londoners. Blue collar, white collar, no collar. None of them looking at me. None of them her.

'Don't look at me.' I turned back to the bar.

'What you say?'

'£27.50 mate,' the barman said. I didn't remember ordering but a neat row of pints stood at attention.

'Right. Yeah.' I slid over three tens, rechecked the crowd. A guy in a red polo had his eyes on me. No. None of them looking at me. None of them her.

Her voice drifted off to sleep with me, several pints' worth of spin in the room and not enough energy even to change out of my clothes. Her voice woke up with me, a summer morning cruel in my eyes and the smell of a flatmate's bacon nauseous in my nose.

'Don't look at me,' it breathed through the window, shifting the curtain. I rolled over, her whisper tickling the back of my neck. 'Please. Don't look at me.'

'Shut up.' I saw her lips blow the words to me like kisses.

'Don't look at me.' I crawled off the bed. Sloughed off my clothes. Met my eyes in the bathroom mirror. 'Please.' Bloodshot. 'Don't look at me.' I brushed my teeth, spitting grease and stale beer. Showered off the sweat. Steam billowed through the bathroom, cooled on the walls to run down cracked tiles like drool over broken teeth, pooled on the floor. I dried myself on a clammy towel. Shrugged on jeans and a t-shirt, sniffed out clean socks and hoofed into my trainers. Checked my watch. Almost midday. Morning had swilled down the drain with the soapy water and somehow I was late. I dug out the essentials; keys, wallet, phone, stowed them in my pockets.

'Don't look at me.' I turned. The hallway behind me was empty. A clack of cutlery on plates and a low hum of chatter from the kitchen, but the corridor, the stairs and the landing above were dark. The text alert of my phone almost shot me out of my skin. *U cming or wht?* I turned back to the door, reached for the handle. 'Don't look at me.' My spine rattled, my palms tingled. I shook my head and opened the door.

An old man was staring at me. Behind the low wall between our splintered square of concrete and the road. No, only walking past. Not looking at me. I made for the tube, head on a swivel.

A young mum nodded thanks as I stepped out of the path of her buggy on the narrow pavement. The kid's owl eyes tracking me as he cruised by. Three teenagers propped against a wall like bits of spare timber threw me hooded glares.

'Don't look at me.' I jolted, turned. No one behind me. I scanned the street. Tall old man with cane. Nondescript middle-age guy. Two pre-teen girls. Woman with black dog. Woman with little boy in baseball cap. I conjured the sweeping beams of their sight lines like searchlights combing the speckled pavements, flinching when they neared me, my teeth beginning to grind. I found, when I tried to start walking, that I had to force myself.

I rounded the corner and crashed into a slender woman in running clothes. She stumbled, caught herself. Hooked an earphone out of one ear.

'Watch it!' She glared at me. She danced around me and resumed her run, casting a last halogen glance over her shoulder. I rolled on under the ground, shoulders high.

There were more people underground. More eyes. Two for each human. More embedded in the tiled sky; cyclops eyes, black and unblinking, all-seeing. The oily brush of their attention felt like ants crawling in my hair. A pulse of warm air foretold the train, which followed behind like a giant steel centipede huffing and panting and jostling with the effort and thrill of carrying so many people so far and so fast. We climbed aboard and I sank into a seat, reaching for the silent anonymity of trains, but the old woman opposite was gazing at me through a pearly film of age.

In one vulture's claw she clutched a blue and white striped plastic bag, and despite the boiler room subway heat she wore so many layers they obscured her entire form. I fancied she sat cross-legged on the seat like an unruly child, a secret from all save me, and I almost laughed. As if hearing my thoughts, she grinned. Red lips, like the bands in a milksnake's skin. My world spiralled inward to the single point of those lips, the wet ivory keys of her teeth behind them. The stark, black space of a missing canine stared like the blown pupil of a drunken third eye. She laughed.

The sound brought the world roaring back. I looked up. Every single eye in the carriage was fixed on me. The lights flickered out as the train slowed for a station. I searched the darkness, after-images of staring eyes hovering in the air like the retina-burns of dead fireworks. Our centipede skittered and rattled into the stop, wheezed to a halt. The lights burst back to life. No one looked at me. I studied every face. Nothing. Vague, sanitary politeness, everyone shielded by a phone or a newspaper. I sat back, breathed deep, then looked up. Red lips, like the films of my eyelids closed against the sun, but the rest of the face? Not old anymore. Young. Blonde hair, a gold rope lying over her shoulder. The muscles in my legs seized against my will, punching me to my feet at the same instant our train coughed, jumped into motion and threw me sideways into a pole. I grabbed for it, caught it, crutched myself on it. The lights stuttered and died again. One second, two seconds, three. I stared at the place I knew she was, hidden from me by the velvet black. Four seconds, five. The light above her flared. She was unchanged. Unmoved. She didn't smile. She spoke. One by one the other lights in the train came on.

'Please. Don't look at me.' The words dripped from me as, spiked through the chest with dread, I turned back to the carriage. Every single gaze was fixed on me. The weight of them pressed on me like hands. I squeezed my eyes shut against them and begged the train to hurry. The grinding clank of a machine's turning-wheel heartbeat pulsed in my head. A screech and a tilt told of a bend. The mellow voice of the announcer claimed the next station was Embankment and we started to slow. I waited, listening for the two-tone chime that'd tell me the doors were opening, and the low, whooping swish when they did. I dragged myself up the pole. I waited. We stopped. The doors opened. The human tide surged and shifted as the train vomited passengers. I opened my eyes. I ran.

'Don't look at me. Don't look at me,' I muttered, over and over as I carved a path through the swarm of people.

I stopped. Before me, facing me, stood the young woman, exempt from the flow of bodies like a standing rock in a river bed.

'Hey, love. Show us that pretty smile,' she said. Red lips, like the guts of a cherry pie. As one, the people filling the station stopped walking, and turned their eyes on me. Twitching, scratchy unease rose up, flooding me with fever from the inside. Sweat pricked my skin. Exhausted, ashamed, I began to cry.

'Oh God,' I said, on a sigh that whistled out between my teeth. 'God. I'm sorry. Alright. I'm sorry.' My eyes drifted shut, I bent my head. I sunk to my knees. 'I'm sorry.'

'I believe you,' she whispered, her breath cold on my forehead. My eyes flicked open, my head snapped up. The station was empty. She bent and laid a kiss between my brows, in the place where the third eye is said to live.

Monday saw me and Sergei back in the cab of the van. Prawn cocktail on his fingertips this time. Women, as always, on his mind.

'That one? Bet you all the money in my pockets there's nothin' under that.' He aimed a corner of the pink foil packet at a woman in a tight skirt, laughing crumbs into the air. The words rose up in my throat, took form in my mouth, waited on my tongue. *Hey, love, show us that pretty smile.*

∾ the end ∾

ABOUT THE AUTHOR

A graduate of Oxford and Columbia Universities, Lauren Everdell was born in London, lived for a while in New York, and now calls the Cotswolds home. At 28, she's set her sights on a career as an author and works towards her great big dreams under the watchful supervision of her chocolate Labrador, Fable.

www.ubiquitousbooks.com

The Beholder was one of the three major prize winning stories.

Feta with Watermelon

Sozou-Kyrkou Konstantina

'Agatha! Agatha! Come quickly! Where are you, Agatha?' Mum's voice comes out in sharp, hoarse cries that stab my deep sleep. I pop out of bed and stumble all the way through the corridor to her bedroom. She's lying face down on the floor, her head stuck under the double bed. 'He's not here,' she says.

Torrential rain, thunder and lightning make a raid against our house. Fat rain drops falling on the balcony rails sound as if kids are stoning them from the street. I place my hand on her back and say, 'Mum, get up, come on.'

'Which part don't you understand, Agatha?' Her face is flushed, her eyes round. 'His slippers aren't here. Where did he go in such a hell of a storm? He'll catch his death. God!' She sits on the parquet, legs spread open, head in palms, like a little girl who's lost her doll. 'You know what a bad cough he's got. His robe isn't here either. He'll soak to the skin.' She kneels, holds on to the bed and sits on it with a groan.

'Mum, take it easy. Dad isn't here.'

She stares at me as if talking to Stan Laurel himself. 'Is that so? What have I been telling you all this time?'

'He doesn't live with us anymore, Mum. Remember?'

Her eyes roll towards the ceiling, her jaw drops. 'What do you mean? Where does he live?'

I sit next to her and caress her back. 'Haven't I told you that he lives with Takis for a while, to keep him company, now that he's divorced?'

'Takis divorced? When?'

'Some months ago.'

Tears well up her eyes. 'My Takis? And your father? When's he coming?'

'When things calm down.' I glance at the clock on the wall. Ten to seven. 'Go to bed now. Come on.'

'I can't sleep.'

I push the slippers her way and help her put them on. 'Come on, let's go to the kitchen then, have something to drink.'

'No. You go to bed. I'll have some water.'

I follow her to the kitchen. She turns on the tap and wets her face. She fills a glass and has a sip. The rain sounds like machine gun bullets against the windowpane.

'Why don't we cook something?' I say. 'What would you like to have right now?'

'Feta with watermelon,' she says and sits on the wooden chair across from me.

I laugh. 'What a funny idea. Sweet with salty?'

'In the summer afternoons we often have feta with watermelon, your father and I. You haven't bought any in a long time.'

'It's Christmas time, Mum. In the summer I will.'

'Christmas, eh?'

'What about an omelette? With chips and feta?'

She claps her hands. 'I love omelettes.' But then she rests her right hand on the table, makes circles with her index finger and says, 'Let's have soup instead. It'll warm your father up when he comes.'

'OK. Soup it is, then.' I stand up and open the cupboard next to the window.

'Don't you think we should call him, see how he's doing? I haven't seen his mobile phone. He must've taken it with him.'

I'm looking for the rice. 'They'll be sleeping now, Mum. We can't call now.'

'Who?'

'Takis and Dad.'

'Oh, yes. Don't use rice, use this … that's like wheat …'

'Risoni, you mean.' I lift the packet and she points to it, jumping in her seat.

'That's it, yes. Your father swallows it better.' She cups her mouth with her hand and says through her fingers, 'No, no, you'd better use the other one that looks like hair; what's its name?'

'Vermicelli, you mean,' I say.

'Yes, this. He swallows it best.'

I pour some water and olive oil in a pot, add some salt and a cube of vegetable broth and let them boil. 'We've got time for a crossword puzzle,' I say and grab a magazine from the pile on the work surface and hand it over to her. She leafs through it. 'They're becoming harder and harder every day. Why do I have to do these, Agatha?'

'Because you have to. They'll help you out.' I show her a small crossword puzzle. 'Come on. Let's do this.' I give her a pen and her glasses.

'But, it's stupid. Look here! Silent cat, two letters.' She glances at me over the dark rim of her spectacles. 'Is there such a thing as a silent cat? Two letters? They all meow and scratch and knock things over and–'

'It means without the vowels, Mum.'

'Ah, no vowels. Which are the vowels?'

I shrug. 'I'll explain later. Pick something else.'

115

She places her finger on another box with clues. She reads slowly, 'What happened yesterday. What does it mean?'

'I don't know. Bygones? Forgotten?'

'F – o – r – g – o – t – t – e – n,' she spells. The pen slides its nose over the empty boxes. 'No, no, six letters only. Got it! Former. That's easy.' She points to the pot. 'The water's boiling.'

I get up, empty the vermicelli into the pot and stir with a ladle.

'When it's done, serve some to your father.'

The rain is driving me up the wall. And I can't stand this headstrong wind that doesn't seem to be willing to let up. It howls and threatens and forces the rain to lash at the windowpanes with all its might. Not even the extractor hood can cover the noise.

When I serve the three plates of soup and the three spoons, her eyes clap on Dad's spoon. 'Agatha, bring one of those we drink juice with, what's it called, a string, a straw, for your dad. He sips it better.'

I hesitate. I look at her and wait. I consider telling her that we're out of straws, but she's waiting too. Doesn't have a spoonful unless she sees the straw on the table. I place it next to Dad's plate. She stares at it, stretches her arm, picks it up, clasps it like a precious pen that's out of ink, but which she cannot part with. Then I see her tear. It wells on her pursed lips, rolls on to the straw, drops into the hot soup she hasn't touched.

I snatch the straw and say, 'Mum, it's eight. What do you say we go to Vasilopoulos, that huge supermarket at Elliniko? They'll have watermelons there. They've got everything.'

Her eyes light up. 'Feta with watermelon! Perfect!'

'Have some soup first and then we leave.'

She bends over her plate and has some hasty spoonfuls. The vermicelli hangs from her lips like strings of phlegm. She wipes her mouth with her sleeve and springs to her feet. 'I'll go get ready.'

By the time I've put on my boots, she's already popped out in front of me in a green, short-sleeved, cotton dress and her blue moccasins. 'I can't find my sunglasses, the black ones, you know. Have you seen them?'

I pull her coat from the hanger and help her put it on. 'You don't need them yet, Mum.'

I open the door. We both stare at the greyish sky, the rain has finally stopped. She hugs me and says, 'You're right, Agatha. I don't need my black glasses. What would I do without you?' At the gate, hand on the handle, she stops short. 'Where are we going?'

'To the supermarket, for watermelon, remember?'

She rubs her hands together in anticipation and says, 'Feta with watermelon. Perfect!' She laughs like a little girl whose mum has finally let her go out in the yard after a rainy day, let her moccasins splash in the water puddles, watch the pieces of herself reflected in them and the warm sun rising above the clouds.

∾ the end ∾

ABOUT THE AUTHOR

Konstantina Sozou-Kyrkou lives in Athens, Greece with her husband and two kids. She has studied literature and holds an MA in Creative Writing from Lancaster University. Her stories (written either in English or in Greek) have been published in many literary magazines and anthologies, some of which having won in competitions.

Feta with Watermelon was shortlisted and highly commended by the judges.

Daughters of the Frost World

Ulla Susimetsä

The pack is about to move. I stagger to my feet. Why did no one wake me? Maybe they let me sleep out of pity ... maybe not.

Pain walks with me. Limping, pushing against the freezing wind, I tail the others across the icy plain. Only the pack matters. The old and the sick are abandoned. They're only more mouths to feed and there's never enough food.

I can no longer hunt, fight, or bear children. One day, the pack won't wait. Birds with wings dark as the night will pick my pain-worn bones clean.

Brunt lifts a hand. We stop. A lonely figure lopes across the ice-covered fjord. From under the fur hood peek ashy strands of hair.

'A frostfur,' Brunt grumbles.

'No threat to us.'

'No, but he might carry something valuable.'

Brunt barks a command. Howling, we run to surround the stranger. A spear smacks him across his shoulders. He drops to his knees, clutching a sack he carries as if he valued it more than his life.

The packs fight each other for hunting grounds. A lonely wanderer is unwelcome, vulnerable.

Another blow. Blood bursts forth, forms startlingly bright patterns on the snow.

Interfering wouldn't help, and what could I do anyway? I carry the old wooden staff – although wood is hard to come by, they still respect me enough not to take it from me while I live. But if I tried using it for a purpose other than steadying my steps … all would see how frail I've become.

The man drops the sack and slumps to the ground. Something tumbles from the sack and falls open. It reveals small snowy fields with marks like those left by a tiny bird. Patterns that glow like blood or like my daughters' sky-bright eyes. I've never seen anything like it.

My youngest daughter, Millie, leaps forward and grasps the thing.

'Give it to me,' Brunt snaps.

'What is it?' Gritty, my oldest daughter, asks and leans in for a closer look. 'Doesn't smell like food.'

'If you can't eat it or fight with it, it's useless,' Brunt huffs.

'Looks dry.' Gritty touches the thing. 'We could burn it.'

'No!' Millie clasps it to her chest.

'Give it up, Millie,' Brunt says. 'It's too heavy for you to carry.'

'No.' My quiet, unsmiling daughter stares at her treasure. I've never seen her like this: her cheeks burning, her eyes aflame.

Brunt moves to take the thing but, as always, Gritty comes to her sister's rescue. 'Let her have it,' she sighs. Gritty is Brunt's mate, a skilled hunter with good childbearing hips. It must be on her orders that the pack hasn't abandoned me yet.

Brunt shrugs. The stranger has other things on him, more valuable: a knife, furs, dried meat.

Soon the pack moves again. We leave the man where he lies, his naked flesh as pallid as snow.

'Who is he? Where did he come from?' Millie looks back over her shoulder.

'Who cares?' I'm more puzzled by the curiosity this small, listless child expresses about the stranger.

Night falls. After trailing a herd of reindeer all day, we've dug our sleeping burrows in the snow and covered them with hides. Our days are an endless struggle for survival, but now there's fresh meat cooking on the fire.

Millie takes out her new treasure. She handles it clumsily but with a hunger in her eyes. I move closer. The thing draws me like the warmth of the fire. I touch the pale fields where the small marks run.

'What is it? Do you know, mother?'

'I can't remember the word.' I was a child when grandmother told me about the old times, things she'd heard from her grandmother. 'I thought these things vanished, like so much else.' When the endless winter came and snow and ice buried the world. Those who adapted to the harsh, frozen desert survived. For generations now, our pack has moved on the snow plains, following game, hunting seal and fish that dwell under the ice.

'What's it for?' Millie asks.

'I believe you can … understand it … that it can tell you something.'

'What does that mean?'

'If you know these signs, they speak to you.' It was just one of grandmother's tales, I always thought, wonderful and wild and impossible. *Marks on a dead tree that let people hear words, see worlds.*

It was a different world once. People had time and strength to spare for things other than survival; things of beauty, things one could see in one's mind but not touch, as strange as that sounds. This thing is of that world.

'They speak to you?'

'Tell a story. Or pass on knowledge.'

'So people made these? To … share thoughts? Make them last?' Millie's eyes sparkle.

And I see a glimpse of what she sees. Beyond this cruel, cold world opens another, different one.

We remember something of the world that once was, but with every generation buried under the snow our knowledge grows less, our memories weaken. We have no way of holding on to them. Even stories lose meaning and are forgotten. The pack is ever on the move, and our tracks are wiped away as if we never existed. But the people who once lived, they left behind things like these.

Were they different from us who fight to live from one cold night to the next, who are driven solely by our hunger and need not to freeze to death?

They're no good to us, of course, these old symbols and the ancient wisdom they might or might not hold. We can't understand them. This unforgiving frost world is all my children and their children will ever know.

'Where did the stranger get this?'

'You're wasting your time! Put that thing away,' Gritty says.

'I want to understand it.' Millie's slim fingers caress the dark marks. 'If I try hard enough–'

'I don't think it's that easy.'

'How would you know? You haven't seen one before, have you? Why couldn't I learn to hear what it says?'

'You just want attention,' Gritty scoffs.

'Me? Which of us always brags about her hunting skills?' Millie sneers. Gritty and I stare: she's never talked back to her sister before. 'So strong and brave and mother's favourite!'

'Oh, but you're the baby she'd still carry if she could. Where'd you be without her? You can't hunt or even defend yourself. Small weakling ... Did you know,' Gritty leans closer, 'that when you were born, mother was told to leave you in the snow to die? That you'd be a burden to the pack.'

Millie turns to me. 'Is it true, mother?' she whispers.

'Yes, but ...' I couldn't do it. I cradled her, still smeared with birth-blood and slime, against my warm skin, fed her every precious drop of milk from my breasts. I do not regret what I did, or failed to do.

Yet, because of this one weakness, I carry a fear much more merciless than the ache in my bones.

'While you play, Millie, I'll hunt. At least I'll be useful.' Gritty stomps away.

For her I never worried. It is not for her sake that I struggle along with the pack despite the crippling pain.

Millie's mouth moves silently as she stares at the thing. The hold of this dead, useless item over her unnerves me, and yet ... I fall under its spell, too. Every night she takes the thing and opens it. She tries to look at it in secret, but in the dark that is impossible. If we light a fire, she sits close to it. The others stare, first suspicious, then curious. We gather around the thing with its wondrous, vivid images, and admire them late into the night.

When we finally break camp, the sun is high already and we move slowly, tiredly. The prey outruns the weary hunters. That night, there is nothing but leathery strips of dry meat to chew.

But again Millie takes out the thing. Everyone moves closer.

'You should put it away,' I whisper.

'I will, soon. Don't fret, mother.'

My youngest has never spoken to me so; I am the caregiver, the one who provides comfort.

'Leave that,' Brunt barks. 'To survive we must hunt, not waste our strength on useless things.'

'Don't call it useless just because we don't understand it. It could say something valuable.'

No one speaks. No one would ever have thought that Millie would challenge Brunt.

His eyes narrow. Before the astonishment grows into admiration towards Millie, he says, 'Give that to me.'

'No!' She clutches the thing in her arms.

'I said, give it to me. It only brings trouble. Gritty was right, we should burn it.' Brunt reaches for the thing. Looking up at him, Millie trembles but bares her teeth and clings to the thing like one surrounded by a hostile pack clings to a weapon.

Everyone freezes. No one defies the leader. That is the absolute, unbreakable rule, necessary for the pack's survival.

Not even Gritty defends her sister now.

Brunt raises his hand. I cry out and move to interfere, but my pain-ridden body is too slow. His palm slaps Millie's cheek.

A stunned silence follows. Brunt grunts, shoves Millie into the snow and wrenches the thing from her grasp. Then, snarling, he flings it into the fire.

The flames leap hungrily. In a few bright moments they've devoured the thing.

Later that night, Millie seeks me out. 'Mother. I must leave.'

'Don't say that! Is it because of Brunt?' She shakes her head. 'Your sister, then? We should've left that thing in the snow! It broke you two apart.' And that must not happen, for when I'm gone, Millie has only Gritty to protect her.

'Mother. When I was born, they told you to leave me behind. To abandon me.'

'But I didn't!' My one act of defiance.

'Still, I never belonged.'

The longing in her eyes is not meant to wound me, but I blame myself. Have I not loved her enough? Given her what she needed?

'Unlike you,' she says, 'unlike Gritty, I have no purpose in the pack. Or in life.'

What purpose should there be! I want to shout. Hunting for food, defending the pack, bearing children – it is all we know.

'Mother, I can't stay, not now that I know there might be … more. I must learn where the stranger came from. If more of those things still exist.'

'Don't be foolish! That might well have been the only one left!' What if it was? And we burned it and now it's gone … why should the loss of it bring me pain?

I don't tell her this. Instead: 'This is our home! You have no idea of where you'd go, the dangers you'd face. Is it worth it? Would you risk your life for it?' For this strange thing, now nothing but ashes; for the faint hope that it might contain … we don't even know what, can barely grasp the idea.

What's more, the pack means strength and safety. Alone, no one lives long. Leaving the pack … it simply is not done.

'I'll go with you.'

We turn to look at Gritty. As Brunt's woman, she's protected us both, her mother and sister. Now she must choose and, unhesitating as always, she's made her decision. Sister over the pack. She has never disappointed me and does not do so now: it's the decision I would have her make.

'Tomorrow, while the others hunt, we leave.'

It's a good plan; they would not let Gritty go, not easily. She's too valuable to the pack.

Come with us. Of course they ask. But they would wait for me, out of love, or out of duty. The pack will not, one day, wait.

With the smooth wooden staff in my hands I sit and watch as they walk away, the only thing left of me once the birds with night-dark wings have picked my bones clean. The fur-clad pair wades in the snow, so certain of their purpose – and yet, if I understand anything, they know so little. We have lost so much.

But they have begun their search and if they survive it … may they find a different world.

∽ the end ∽

ABOUT THE AUTHOR

Ulla Susimetsä is a Finnish writer whose debut novel, co-authored with her husband, Marko, was published in August 2018. Her short stories have appeared in various anthologies and magazines. When she's not writing or reading, she's eating chocolate or wielding her Viking sword.

Daughters of the Frost World was shortlisted and highly commended by the judges.

ABOUT FANTASTIC BOOKS PUBLISHING'S CHARITY ANTHOLOGIES

I have long believed that paying forward is the right way to conduct daily life – personal and business. It was with this in mind that I began creating our charity anthologies. Every one of them donates 10% to a charity of our choosing for the lifetime of the publication.

Releasing charity anthologies is a privilege and is by no means a selfless act. It has allowed us to find some of the best and brightest new writing talent while supporting a worthy cause.

Our first collection, a mix of science fiction and fantasy called Fusion, led to us discovering Drew Wagar who went on to become a best-selling novelist. That first anthology also saw the start of our partnership with the equally prolific Stuart Aken who was an invited contributor. Both authors said they came back to us with their work because of the quality of our editorial process on Fusion. We hope we've maintained that quality in this collection.

Dan Grubb, CEO Fantastic Books Publishing August 2018

We sincerely hope you enjoyed these stories and will get online and let our authors know by leaving them a review on Amazon and Goodreads.

FANTASTIC BOOKS CHARITY ANTHOLOGIES

Fusion – a science fiction and fantasy collection that donates to the World Cancer Research Fund

666 – a horror collection that donates to EDS-UK

Synthesis – a science fiction and fantasy collection that donates to Freedom from Torture

aMUSEing Tales – donates to the WorldWide Orphans Foundation

Ours – donates to the WorldWide Orphans Foundation

Dreaming of Steam – 23 tales of Wolds and rails that donates to the Yorkshire Wolds Railway

You can find more delightful tales and wonderfully woven prose at our Fantastic Books Store.
www.fantasticbooksstore.com